Not Safe, but Good
Volume II

SHORT STORIES SHARPENED BY FAITH

Edited by Bret Lott

THOMAS NELSON
Since 1798

NASHVILLE   DALLAS   MEXICO CITY   RIO DE JANEIRO   BEIJING

Published in Nashville, Tennessee. Thomas Nelson is a trademark of Thomas Nelson, Inc.

Thomas Nelson, Inc. books may be purchased in bulk for educational, business, fund-raising, or sales promotional use. For information, please e-mail SpecialMarkets@ThomasNelson.com.

Publisher's Note: This collection is a work of fiction. Names, characters, places, and incidents are either products of the author's imagination or used fictitiously. All characters are fictional, and any similarity to people living or dead is purely coincidental.

Library of Congress Cataloging in Publication Data

Not safe, but good / edited and with an introduction by Bret Lott.
    p. cm.
    "Volume 1, formerly The best Christian short stories [volume 1]."
    ISBN-13: 978-1-59554-320-2 (v. 1 : softcover)
    ISBN-10: 1-59554-320-1 (v. 1 : softcover)
    ISBN-13: 978-1-59554-275-5 (v. 2 : softcover)
    ISBN-10: 1-59554-275-2 (v. 2 : softcover) 1. Christian fiction, American. 2. Short stories, American. I. Lott, Bret. II. Title: Best Christian short stories.
PS648.C43N68 2007
813'.01083822—dc22   2007012145

Printed in the United States of America

07 08 09 10 11 RRD 5 4 3 2 1

Contents

Introduction

Welcome to the second volume in the annual series begun last year with the publication of *The Best Christian Short Stories*. But, you may well observe, this book you hold in your hands isn't called *The Best Christian Short Stories Volume II*.

Good point.

The change in our title reflects perhaps a better sense of what we are after in putting together a collection each year of the best in contemporary Christian fiction. *Not Safe, but Good* is, of course, taken from C. S. Lewis's *The Lion, the Witch, and the Wardrobe*, and that moment when Lucy inquires of Mr. Beaver as to the nature of Aslan, "Then he isn't safe?" "Safe?" Mr. Beaver replies, "Who said anything about safe? 'Course he isn't safe. But he's good. He's the King, I tell you."

The stories you have in your hand are by no means safe. But they are good. Yet by *good* I don't mean that they are simply written well, or only evocative or thoughtful or redemptive (though they are indeed all of those and more). What is meant here by the word *good* is that the stories are after something deeper than the surface of their tales; they are after seeing as fully and as acutely and as profoundly as possible the human condition in relation to a God who loves us, and who is anything but safe.

Reader be warned: here in this collection you will find stories of doubt, stories of loss, stories of abandonment and failure and betrayal. Unsafe stories.

Precisely the model Christ gave us with His parables.

To illustrate what I think of as the sort of unsafe story in which Christ so often trafficked—that is, the visceral quality of Story He knew so well—we ought to imagine the story of the Good Samaritan taking place in your hometown, maybe over on Sixteenth Street, one block down from the pedestrian mall, where this evening a man has been stabbed and robbed and left to die in the little cubbyhole of a doorway that leads into the shoe repair store over there, a place out of the way and half-hidden for the way shadows from the streetlamp at the corner fall so that no one sees him.

Now we must imagine that the first one to come upon him is a well-known evangelical leader, who is in his motorcade on the way to a rally at the professional baseball team's stadium in the hills just outside the city. We watch this leader tell his driver to slow down, watch him look at this body on the street—and here's the hard part, but necessary all the same so that we can understand the depth of effect Christ's parable had on his listeners—we must *imagine* that this well-known evangelical leader tells the driver to move on, that there is a crusade to get to.

Next we must imagine that, here in this same city on this same night, the next passerby is a bishop, on his way to an international ecumenical gathering at the professional basketball team's complex at the city center downtown. We must imagine that we see the bishop's limousine slow down as well, and that he sees through his tinted window this man in a doorway, dying, and that though he sees him, the bishop, too, has to make his own conference—there are programs to discuss, policies to develop!—and he leaves him there, intent on not letting down the thousands who are gathering at the sports center to concern themselves with the greater issues of our day.

And finally, we have to imagine we see a man walking along that same street, and we have to imagine his seeing a shape in a doorway, a heap of something, angles and darkness in this light from the streetlamp. He sees a spreading pool of black beside this shape—it's a man, he sees, a man!—that pool beside him a shape making itself bigger and darker each second he stands there watching, and we must see this man bend then to the other, and take his pulse, and turn him over, and then look left and right until he spots the Rite Aid at the corner of Sixteenth and Welton, a place he knows he can bring him for a few moments and can get someone to call an ambulance for him. And then the man picks up the one who has been stabbed and carries him quick as he can across the intersection and inside, where there will be help.

But the man, the one who stopped when the others wouldn't. Who is he?

An imam, walking home from the mosque over on thirteenth and Edwards, the Maghrib over a while ago. He lives in an apartment building four more blocks away, and dinner is waiting, as are his three children and wife. But there was business to attend to at the mosque—someone arguing over how to calculate the noon prayer of Zuhr and why that caused the evening prayer, Maghrib, to be off by a minute; a woman showing up at the door as he was locking up, to ask after some money for food—and now he was late. But not too late to save the life of a stranger.

That's the unsafe story Christ might have told, if I may be so bold, to His listeners. And then He would have asked of those Evangelical and Fundamentalist and Catholic and Anglican leaders who had egged Him on in the first place with their smart-aleck question, "Who is my neighbor?"—Christ would have asked of them this: "Which of these three do you think proved to be a neighbor to the man who fell into the robber's hands?"

And they would have had to answer, "The one who showed mercy toward him. The Muslim." And Jesus would have said to them, "Go and do the same."

Christ's stories surprised His listeners. They were un-expected, yet the surprise of them was totally logical and clear and, finally, the kind of surprise that makes good literature good literature: the surprise turn in a story, when the reader must come face-to-face with *himself*, and his own failures, and the dust of his own life, a dust with which we are each of us fully familiar, but which we forget about or ignore or accommodate ourselves to. The dust of our lives that we have grown accustomed to, and which it takes a piece of art created in the spirit of Christ to remind us of ourselves, and our distance from our Creator—and the chasm that is bridged by Grace.

Jesus' stories were brutal, offensive, and visceral, as well as joyful and triumphant: think now of the woman who finds the coin and rejoices!

And it is in this spirit—this Spirit—that the stories collected here are offered: they are meant to be a challenge and are meant to be a blessing. They aren't safe, but they are good.

—*Bret Lott*

The Man Who Said Yellow

by Diane Glancy

Sometimes our presumptions about our relationship to God prove to be our undoing; sometimes our willingness to let go our presumptions about ourselves proves to be the beginning of righteousness. In this story of one artist's nagging vision of what he believes to be God's mission for his life, we see played out the notions of creation, of art, of purpose in his quest to accomplish what he believes is God's will.

—BRET LOTT

1

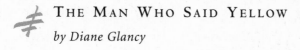

THE MAN WHO SAID YELLOW
by Diane Glancy

> The camel, I had noticed, was passing,
> with great difficulty, through the eye
> of the needle.
>
> — Renata Adler, *Brownstone*

When a great rumble of evangelism swept Brownsville, it left an unswept place around Noe as he worked in his shed. Noe was the artist, the *el artisto*, in his family. Others looked at him that way. Uncles. Cousins. Neighbors would come to look in the shed. Strangers who had heard of Noe would peer in while he worked. Often, Noe was unaware of them. His three sons started going to church with his wife. The house was abuzz with what was happening. The family had been Catholic since the Spanish invasion. Now there was an upstart *iglesia*. A church of their own.

In meetings that lasted into the night, some excitement was there. It was said that angels descended and touched toothaches.

Bursitis, arthritis, and cysts were healed. A baby who had coughed for days was quiet and asleep.

It was the girls that must have been at church, Noe thought. Otherwise his sons would not have been eager to go. His dreams, ah! That was the origin of art. That was his *iglesia.* That was his Maker, his *El Señor* himself—the road of open dreams. It was where he found his *yellow fever.* His *yellow works.* Canary. Finch. Yellow jacket. Noe also went to the Laguna Atascosa Wildlife Refuge. The Wetlands of Boca Chica. The Los Ebanos Preserve—for images of the wild birds, insects, and small animals of his carvings, some of them surreal.

Did not the Maker speak of dreams in the Book his wife, Hesta, read to him? *In a dream, in a vision of the night, he opens the ears of men and seals their instruction.* The Maker was the Maker of dreams, and not the dreams themselves. But Noe did not agree and brushed her aside.

Sometime later, there were three weddings. Not all at once, but over the year at the church, after the courtings and dinners and parties with the families, Roberto married Inez Garcia. Domingo married Cornelia Gomez. Dagoberto married Elee Padillo.

"At least his sons would not marry the daughters of unbelievers. At least they stayed away from the ungodly," Hesta said.

Now that Noe and Hesta were suddenly alone together, they didn't know what to do. Noe kept at work in his shed, carving his wooden pieces, painting them, signing them. The curators fought among themselves for his work. Noe showed his pieces and sold them at the Brownsville Heritage Museum, the Art League Museum, Imagene's Studio, and the Festival Internacional de Otoio in Matamoros across the Mexican border. There had been an article in the Brownsville newspaper about Noe's birds from the center of the earth. Another article followed about Noe's *subterranean cosmos*, his ingenious *mythologies of inner aviaries*. Hesta sent the articles to their relatives who had gone north to Minnesota for work. She sent them to relatives still in Mexico.

Noe's work shed sat on a hill near his house, with its back to the setting sun. Roberto cut a window in the shed for him and let in the evening light. After dark, Noe could work under a lightbulb in a metal reflector that caused the light to burn bright and direct on his work. In the day, when the heat came in the window, Roberto installed a canvas awning.

After several years, no children were born as yet, and the three wives grieved. "There is a reason," Hesta said.

In Noe's dreams, animals began to appear two by two. When he told his wife, she was beside herself. Maybe God was getting hold of her husband at last. Maybe now he would go to church with her, just as she hoped. When Noe's two-by-two dreams continued, Hesta said, "Maybe you'll become a visionary. The end of days must be upon us," she concluded. "There is going to be a flood. Make an ark. Gather animals. That's why there have been no grandchildren."

"This isn't a ship yard," Noe said. "This is the *artisto's* shed with a tin corrugated roof"—where the grackles hopped, making scratching sounds that seemed at times to direct Noe's hands.

"Then make the ark with a tin roof like your shed."

That night Noe heard camels bellow. Muffled but recognizable coming from the distance. Had he fallen asleep in his shed? Wouldn't his wife be coming to wake him or call him to bed? How could he tell? Male and female. That's what they were supposed to do. Multiply. Replenish.

That's what he did as an artist. Populate the barren world with his art.

"Camels. I see camels coming," Noe said again as Hesta took notes. "A camel train. They are bearing weight. They are with merchants, or the merchants are with them."

Eventually Noe's dreams became darker, murkier. Where did his art come from? Though camels were the central theme of his dreams, he also was flooded with images of Mexican cattle, scrawny goats, lizards, snakes, stray dogs, half-starved horses. In spite of it all, he continued work in his shed, three-sided, with the fourth a large door that pushed back so that the front was nearly open to the flat brown hills.

It was as if his dreams, looking into the center of the earth for the birds that flew there, for the animals that burrowed there, had found instead, Hell. What was Hell? What was his definition? His understanding? The absence of dreams and visions? Surely such an important place should have a concept in his mind.

"Hell is when you don't know God," Hesta, his wife, said.

But Noe's theology *was* a man's belief in God. Noe just wasn't enthusiastic and evangelistic. Noe knew the Maker, *El Señor* himself, as Himself, was there to be reckoned with at the end. Noe would live his life, do good where he could find it to do. Be faithful to his work, his art. Love his wife and family, even when he heard Inez, Cordelia, and Elee scrapping.

What else could Hesta's God, her Maker, her *El Señor* himself, want?

Then why these dreams of animals? What was shaping his visions? What journey was ahead? He penciled the shapes from his dreams on a roll of brown paper. He unrolled more of the paper as he drew. He had dreamed more than he realized. What were these shapes? Camels, strange and exotic, he had never seen except in the Brownsville Gladys Porter Zoo.

He felt something was pulling out his eye.

His sons came of an evening with their plates of flautas and refried beans. Roberto and Inez. Domingo and Cornelia. Dagoberto and Elee, who was never ready, always late. Once, Dagoberto arrived without her. She came ambling in later, quiet and subdued, feeling shame. But she had to make certain of everything. Nothing stayed the same for her. It moved. Her shoes. Her little anklets edged with tatting. Whatever she needed, she had to look for. Find. Her world was watery as the Gulf and ever moving. Her dark, sullen eyes moped about the room. What disarray the lives of Dagoberto and Elee would be when the children came. How loose. Unwired.

Noe continued work on his figures, painting them the yellow of a papier-mâché dog he had seen in Mexico—trying to find the essence at the core of yellow. The yellow that turned the eye into it and would not let it go. If he could look straight at the sun—he would know it. He would have it. An electrified yellow. The electrification of yellow. Even the sun could not fade it for years. The sun was what they had in Brownsville. Licking everything dry. Dulling it. The brown hills, the brown land, the bottom of the page, the dropping off into Mexico.

Long ago, he visited his grandparents in a *barrio* south of Matamoros in the Republic of Mexico in their adobe house. Inside his grandparents' house, where the adobe walls were a foot thick, it was cool. The house was built for the heat. Why didn't Noe have an adobe shed for his work place? Why was it a shed made of wood with a tin roof that sat out in the middle of the sun? The heat waves sometimes rose in his eyes. The whole earth wavered with Elee's indecision. What had been there in the relationship with his grandparents?—those brilliant days. The irretrievable—the *unretrievable* past was the ache at the core of yellow.

Noe's grandfather's name had been Lamech. His great-grandfather had lived long enough that he remembered him. Whittling on wood with his bent and swollen fingers, his aching hands. His language the waltz of the Gulf waves. Those days crushed in the past—those words bled yellow in Noe's memory.

The heat of Brownsville. Despite the large ceiling fans in his shed. The canvas awning. Despite the spray of water he hosed over the tin roof in the early evening so he could work after supper when his family had gone to the ongoing revival at the growing church of the new *iglesia*. Where had it come from? Why had it started? Why did it continue?

Noe thought of an ark with rooms for the animals in his visions. A narrow window running the length of the ark, just under the tin roof. One door. A retractable ramp. How would the rain sound when it pecked on the roof? Maybe like a thousand grackles walking there.

Sometimes Noe still was at work in his shed before dawn under the lightbulb in its metal reflector to accentuate the light. Sometimes at noonday, after lunch, he slept in a hammock in the shade of his yard until the heat subsided a degree or two and he could return to his shed as the sun began to dive into the darkness that awaited it. The sun was the originator of light. The clouds were a garment over it. Garments it seldom wore. Usually it was heat and light and more heat and more light in Brownsville.

Besides camels, Noe's dreams continued with coyotes, foxes, wildcats, the fowl, the creeping things. Snakes in abundance. Scorpions. Fire ants. Termites. Brown spiders with the deadly mark of a violin on their back. How slowly he must pass over words, over visions, over those dreams to see what they were about. They were dangerous. Quick.

When sleep falls upon men, in the slumberings upon their beds— He also had a troubling dream of a black angel, a *Being*, that roamed the hills, that had come out of the earth, that had escaped from Hell, that lay in the sun all day because of the coolness compared to Hell that drove everyone mad with thirst. When Noe told his wife, she said it was a black angel, already seen by many in Brownsville. It is what had sent everyone running to church. They were nearly on top of one another, there were so many people crowded together in the small building, and the revival kept growing. What were they going to do? Hesta said the angel was a fugitive from the wars in Heaven, who now lived in the center of the earth, and would have to go back—who had somehow escaped to terrify everyone as long as it was able—and take back as many with it as it could—Just because someone didn't say Jesus Christ was Lord, Hell was laid out for them? Noe asked—unbelievable. Unacceptable—just Jesus without saints and priests and confession booths and candles? But *Jesus alone* was the message his wife, Hesta, brought back from church. Yes. In a dream, Noe saw someone chasing the Virgin Mary off with a broom.

His night visions continued. Bright yellow camels, not the fulvous ones in the Brownsville zoo. What was up? He had *camelitis*, someone said.

What if Noe had to build an ark not for the Flood but the Heat? "What if I dig a cellar? Submerge the ark?" Noe asked his wife one evening, wet with sweat, as they ate burritos in the yard. What if they had to flee from the heat that would flourish, that would rift, that would bake and transform the ingredients of the world? What if he was called to build a submarine? That's what they needed. The subterranean was cooler. Just step into the earth, not deep, but just beneath the surface—weren't Domingo and Cornelia sleeping in their basement that was always cooler? Didn't Roberto and Inez join them on the hottest nights?

In the meantime, Noe wore his carpenter pouch, with his hammer in its cloth notch. He was surrounded in his work shed with metal files, clamps, drills, sandpaper, turpentine, rags, small brushes with bristles hardened with dried paint, chisels, augers, little saws with metal piranha teeth. Whatever it took to file, to whack, to form. Tubes of yellow paint, some of the letters covered with paint, which made the tubes read, *low*, *el*, and others simply, *yel*.

Noe also built insect cages, aviaries for an imaginary ark. He drew plans for stalls for other animals, glass cages for the creeping snakes. What was this dry flood?

El Señor had given exact measurements and Noe had not written them down. There Noe was *sombrero dancing* in his dreams. He was at the 1840s' Palo Alto Battlefield National Historical Site near Brownsville. Noe was at war. He was brushed with the history of the Mexican-American War that changed the shape of both countries.

The earth was filled with violence, hunger, and need. That was a clue. It was a game of Clue he had played as a boy. The game had been in Spanish. His grandfather, Lamech, had given him the game in English, so he could learn the language he needed to learn. What clue was *El Señor* giving?

God was giving hints in Noe's dreams, and Noe was losing them. His wife put paper and a pencil beside his bed. "Wake me," she said. "I'll take notes. I will do the writing. But I need measurements. Instructions. Why would they be given to you who work in your shed instead of coming to church with us? Tell me what you see." But Noe's dreams were like someone talking from underwater.

One door. Windows at the top. A tin, corrugated roof. Grackles scratching there.

Word got out. Somehow Hesta let it slip. Noe was having visions of camels, and other animals, two by two. The church went wild. Cornelia said it was an aviary itself. Inez said they all would want in. How could he build an ark big enough?

His shed was an ark, wasn't it? A place of refuge in the flood of family and world events. He had sanctuary. He had replenished. But once the Flood started—if there was going to be a Flood—would they all try to crowd in his work shed as Inez said? Was it the black angel playing tricks? Was it a ghost whose purpose was to confuse?

What was he supposed to do? Noe built birds, not arks. He sat by his lightbulb in its metal reflector. The insects swarmed. Did they know they would die unless they could keep flapping their wings for as long as the Flood remained? No, the rain on their wings would bring them down.

"Doors tall enough for the camels," Cornelia said.

"And the giraffes," Elee said.

Noe hadn't thought of them. And of course doors wide enough for the elephants.

What would they do as they sat in the ark, surrounded by the beasts, the fowl, the creeping things? Was that what *El Señor* wanted? In Noe's night visions, the whole town sat crowded together in the ark as they waited for the rising waters. Weren't the icebergs melting and would raise the sea level? Wasn't the sea coming up to claim the land? Yes, the Gulf would rise. It would cover the Rio Grande. It already was rising, and no one knew what to do. Nightmares and Hell were giving evidence of themselves. Was the overpopulation of grackles everyone noticed like the gathering of bad spirits ready for an impending decimation? How long would they float in a Flood? But what if Noe built an ark and there was no Flood? What if, after Noe's death, his sons used the ark for a bait shop for fishermen on the Gulf shore? What if his dreams were a deluge he couldn't stop?

But there was not supposed to be another Flood. He remembered there was a promise of some sort. But Hesta seemed unconcerned.

In the night, Noe could hear the black angel rip the hills with its teeth, the mad *Being* that escaped from Hell in the center of the earth. In the afternoons, Noe walked the brown hills. Would he be the last to catch on like Elee, his daughter-in-law? As he walked the hills in despair, he was stopped as an *illegal*, but the border patrol brought him home and Hesta testified he was a citizen and her husband. Despite his family's fear of the black angel, Noe continued to walk the hills following the quavering heat waves, this time with identification. He roamed for weeks. His feet swelled. Bushes scratched his arms. His face sunburned. His children pleaded with him. When would God let her husband go, Hesta thought?

Then the Maker, *El Señor* himself, appeared, wearing a yellow poncho. For a while *He* watched the hawks. The falcons. The predators. The helicopters from the border patrol. *He* listened to the upset world with its waters rising. Once in a while, Noe looked at *El Señor*, waiting for the Maker to speak. Soon, *El Señor* announced that Hell was dreams and visions without *El Señor* attached. The Maker said he had waited for Noe to speak to *Him*. He wanted to tell Noe that he had confused his own dreams with the Maker's, the giver of dreams, just like his wife had said. What would float then was a work shed, an ark of clear vision. Noe's art was still his oar, his only hope—But if Noe would listen to the Maker's dreams—it was not an ark that *El Señor* wanted—it was a church *He* wanted Noe to build. "I want you to paint it the yellow of your birds and animals," God said, rubbing his fingers together. "I saw your work at Imagene's and the Heritage Museum. I knew I wanted it for one of my churches." It was Noe's yellow that had drawn the Maker like fly paper.

Was it all a fluke? Or had the Creator spoken to Noe on the ankle bone of America? Yes, that was Brownsville. No, the foot bone, the toe bone just across the North American border. God had the gumption to come, then leave as quickly as He had appeared—with a trail of burros in his wake. For a moment the sky seemed to open to let *El Señor* and his burros back into Heaven, and Noe saw a light that sliced his eyes like a carving knife until he closed them.

Noe had misplaced *El Señor* in his own head where the Maker was supposed to swim on the floodwater of Noe's thoughts. Yes, Noe had seen himself as Creator. The Great and Old One. Noe fell down on his knees in the floodwaters of regret. When Noe returned to work in a heated fervor, the canvas awning blew up in a sudden storm-wind and the work shed looked like it had a sail—the townsfolk came to watch. They knew Noe had a vision. What was he building? No, he was drawing—he was drawing plans for their church. In the end, *El Señor* was going to enlarge the *iglesia*—it's what they prayed for, Hesta reminded them. Noe saw the dimensions in his dream. This time he wrote them down. Noe, the repentant *artisto*, would be used to build a church or draw it and show others how to build or help build. The animals in his dreams had been the people, burden bearers, workers, men and women who carried the weight of their families—also the hungry, the sick, those who needed sanctuary, those who had been scorpions—who had wounded others and now sought redemption.

The ark was *El Señor Himself*, his wife said as the family gathered with their stuffed peppers, their chili rellenos, and refried beans. Sometimes mystery turned up like a canvas awning. The ark was a type, a metaphor for safety on the *floodwaters* of the world. Once in an everlasting while, some dust blew up in the heat, stirred by the winds from heaven, and left a puddle of revelation—a downpour of sorts on a level Noe had not expected, nor even desired.

DIANE GLANCY was awarded a 2003 National Endowment for the Arts Fellowship and the 2003 Juniper Poetry Prize from the University of Massachusetts Press for *Primer of the Obsolete*. Her novels include *Designs of the Night Sky*, *Stone Heart: a Story of Sacajawea*, and *Pushing the Bear, the 1838–39 Cherokee Trail of Tears*. She recently completed a novel about a Christian's experience with Alzheimer's, *No Word for the Sea*, and is completing *The Uprising of Goats, Portraits of Biblical Women*. She received her MFA from the University of Iowa and is a professor at Macalester College in St. Paul, Minnesota, where she has taught Native American Literature and Creative Writing.

Block Island

by Thomas Lynch

Sometimes it's best to let the story reveal itself to the reader, rather than preface it with words from an editor. Such is the case with this moving tale of one man's journey.

—BRET LOTT

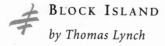

BLOCK ISLAND
by Thomas Lynch

It was *Good Riddance* that put Adrian Littlefield on the lecture circuit. Before *Riddance* he'd self-published a couple pastel covered self-help books with fashionably gerundive titles— *Learning to Love in the Present Tense* and *Making the Best of the Worst Case Scenarios.* They were widely ignored and only sold to his family and folks at the church where he youth-pastored back in those early years of marriage and parenthood. He'd done a workbook on dividing family duties between spouses and written a couple of articles for the ministerial press but otherwise was going nowhere and barely making ends meet until, after she left him, he wrote *Good Riddance—Divorcing for Keeps* and it changed his life.

It held that some divorces, like some marriages, are made in heaven. And we ought to be thankful for them. The key to living in concert with God's Will or the Natural Order or what the Fates had in mind for you was to learn to accept the direction your love life was taking you in, even when it meant the end of love. Divorce was neither the result of too much of one thing nor too little of another, too many heartbreaks or too few. It was, like tsunamis and famines, hurricanes and genocides, God's way of culling humanity's herd of lovers, for reasons that were unknowable to mortals, but part, nonetheless, of a larger plan. Crap happens—Adrian Littlefield told his readers unambiguously—we must go with the flow. That's life, get over it, get on with it.

It took him three weeks to write it, a month to get an agent, and another month to get a contract and a fat advance from a publisher in New York. It was an immediate hit. The first printing sold out in a week. The paperback rights went for a quarter million.

The invitations followed. He worked up a little forty-minute shtick for the keynotes and workshops. He could bend his presentation, peppered with tastefully suggestive humor, around the occupational curiosities of any professional association. He had an infomercial—one of those hour-long specials where he wore baggy clothes and did a little chalk talk with a really attractive and earnest-looking studio audience—in postproduction. He traveled three months out of every four from his home office in Findlay, Ohio, where he housed, next to his Victorian farm house, in a barn he'd refurbished with money from his books, The Center for Post Marital Studies—an elaborate tax shelter, along with the Foundation that raised funds to advance the work of the CPMS, which was primarily to pay its principal apostle—himself—to spread the word such as it was revealed to him. Some nights, posting the latest newsletter to the web site, or linking a recent interview so his followers could listen in, he felt not a little like Paul writing to the various churches. If, as that great circuitrider wrote, it is better to marry than to burn, was it not much better still to divorce than to smolder? "Ex's" Adrian's favorite slogan held, "You can't live with 'em and you can't shoot 'em. A little *Good Riddance* goes a long way."

In the years since *Riddance* was released, he'd written *The Good Riddance Workbook* and *Questions & Answers About Good Riddance,* thereby giving the trilogy his publisher said really would saturate the market. The more offers that came into the CPMS, the more he raised his fees for speaking, which had the effect of making him seem worth that much more, which brought, of course, more offers. He counted it an irony, and a pleasant one, that he'd become de facto an itinerant preacher— the calling he'd felt early and often in his youth—albeit preaching a secularized gospel that was a hybrid of pop-psych, warm fuzzies, personal witness and cultural study. That he homilized not from the pulpits of great cathedrals but from the lecterns of convention hotels struck him as part of the Creator's plan for him. He'd stopped saying "Gawd" in the deeply reverential tone of his Methodist training and taken rather to the user-friendly, guilt-free parlance of nature and creation. It was, he told himself, more "inclusive." Also it paid better. Likewise he'd given up "The Reverend" for simply "Doctor" Adrian Littlefield for the scholarly, vaguely medicinal ring that it added to his brief. He had a D.D. mail order from one of the agencies that advertised in clergy magazines and an honorary doctorate from his alma mater, Bowling Green University, where he'd given the commencement speech the year after his book came out. He was certainly not the first to observe that the high priests of the current culture had secular rather than sacred credentials. Not lost on him either was the happy fact that divorcing, formerly seen as a failure, had been the essential key to his success. Though the scandal cost him his job as the longsuffering and underpaid youth pastor at the Findlay United Methodist Church, as soon as his wife "left" him, he became the tragically abandoned single father of two kids under ten. Once the book came out, with excerpts published in *Redbook* and *Esquire*, interviews on public radio, profiles on prime-time network shows, he'd become a kind of local hero. He even did a sit-down with Oprah to chat and answer the audience questions, which appearance alone had accounted for a massive third printing of *Riddance* and an audio book.

When he found himself, as he often did, disembarking from some posh hotel, with the hefty stipend of his speaking fee cooling in his briefcase, the limo idling at curbside, waiting to take him to the plane, the appreciation of conventioneers ringing in his ears, and a young woman waking in the bed in the suite upstairs to find him gone but not, he could convince himself, entirely forgotten, Adrian Littlefield's heart filled with thanksgiving for the failure he had made of his marriage. "All things," he told himself, "work together toward some good." If God was a practical joker, well then he would grin and bear it. He offered, in such moments, silent and abundant thanks and praise to Whomever Was In Charge and might be out there, wherever, listening to his heart of hearts.

It was the National Association of Family Law Attorneys (NAFLA) annual meeting in Connecticut that brought him to the Foxwoods Casino—a high-stakes bingo parlor parlayed by the Mashantucket Pequot Tribal Nation into one of the most profitable gaming parlors in the country. It rose out of the hilly forests between Norwich and the coast, like something out of Kubla Khan, its lights blazing in the darkness, a pleasure dome on the "rez."

"Eighty-six thousand dollars an hour, twenty-four hours a day, 365 days et cetera," the limo driver who met his flight in Hartford said. "That's how much they net in profit. Pretty good revenge, eh? We gave them firewater and reservations, they give us Keno and the dollar slots. They don't call it wampum for nothing."

The shops and restaurants and conference center and hotel all played into the tribe's master plan of revenge—to disabuse as many of their oppressors of as much money as possible in the most mindless way. It seemed a suitable locale for the divorce attorneys to hold their annual meeting. Dr. Littlefield was the keynote speaker. His fee was fifteen thousand, first-class travel, ground transport, premium lodging and meals. His books and videos sold briskly after his lectures. He signed them "Best Wishes—A.L." and if the purchaser were a divorced woman of a certain age and style he'd add, "every available benevolence." He thought this sounded a literary chord, and while what he wrote was far from literary, he thought the pretence would do no harm.

In most cases he would fly into a venue the night before, check in, order a chicken salad from room service, watch a movie and go to bed. He would be up early the next morning to walk, then ready himself for his standard forty-minute speech, fifteen minutes of Q&A and whatever it took to sign all the books. Then he'd make for the airport and the next venue.

But this conference was in late July, in a resort casino near the sea in New England. He'd been going nonstop for most of the year and the pictures in the pre-registration packet looked inviting. There was a "Traditional Yankee Clambake" scheduled at Mystic Seaport, the usual golf outing and "A Day on Beautiful Block Island." He'd never been to Block Island but he had kept a picture of the place in his imagination for years. The brochure photo of handsome couples assembled around fruity drinks, smiling from the porch of an elegant Victorian hotel caught his eye. He told the organizers he'd be staying for the entire conference and while he wouldn't golf with the attendees, he'd be happy to eat with them and wanted to take the trip to the island. They were happy to book him two more nights in the suite, knowing that their members would be pleased at the chance to visit with the renowned expert.

The tour bus from Foxwoods to Pt. Judith took an hour. The boat from Pt. Judith to Block Island took another—thirteen miles across Block Island Sound from Galilee, RI to the town of New Shoreham at the Old Harbor. Stepping aboard the car ferry *Anna C.*, Dr. Adrian Littlefield tried to imagine what crossing water must have added to the romance his former spouse must have felt en route to the first of her several assignations. He took a seat on the middle deck of the ferry among the conferees from NAFLA, who sat in a block in the first few rows of benches, careful to get an aisle seat for the escape he planned once the boat was on its way. They waited for cars and day-trippers to board, admiring the small fleet of fishing vessels in Pt. Judith. The *Enterprise* and *Lady Helen* and *Stormy Elizabeth*—it was not so much the names as the black riggings and booms and spools of netting that put him in mind of life's entanglements. He thought he might begin another series of books entitled *Life's Entanglements.*

"*Good Riddance* was a miracle for me! I have to tell you, Doctor . . ."

"Oh, thank you"—he smiled at the red-haired woman sitting next to him—"that's very flattering."

"No, really, Doctor. It gave me permission to . . . I hope I'm not interrupting your . . ."

"No, no, not at all. I'm glad you liked it."

"I mean before your book I never would have, you know, felt empowered." She emphasized the middle syllable of "empowered" like she had "permission."

"Yes, yes," Adrian said and looked deeply into her blue eyes trying to imagine what idiom from the lexicon of daytime talk shows she would give out with next, a scrutiny which the red haired woman mistook for interest.

"Of course, there's so much baggage we had to let go of first, my ex and me, before we could, you know, grow up and grow apart, you know, together."

Adrian nodded and smiled and stood and took her hand and held it meaningfully before looking about as a man does looking for the nearest toilet.

"Too much java," he said, to explain himself, and the man next to the red haired woman pointed toward the rear of the ferryboat where they all had boarded.

"Head's at the back, Dr. Littlefield, we'll save your spot."

Adrian smiled and made his move to the back of the boat just as it was disembarking and climbed the stairs up to the open upper deck.

Block Island was the site of his former wife's first infidelity. He'd only ever seen it in pictures—photos she'd brought home from her trip to New York that April, ostensibly to visit her friend Christina. "I just need to get away from Findlay, and family and kids," she told him, "just for a week, a little perker-upper. Christina has taken the time off of work, we're going to do girl things." Clare was thirty-three at the time. They had a son and a daughter, ages eight and four. They'd been married almost eleven years. Her discontent was palpable.

"Oh, Ben invited us out to the island for the weekend," she told him when she returned from the week away, leaving him with the children and the house and his own work to manage. "You remember Ben, don't you? Uncle Harold's friend. The artist, you know, Harold and Olive's neighbor. Christina and I ran into him in town at the studio and he invited us out to the island for the weekend. We couldn't get theater tickets so we decided to go. Harold and Olive were going to come too but cancelled at the last minute."

Adrian remembered the determinedly plural references and the way it was supposed to work against his suspicions. And the supposed serendipity of it all, all very last minute and carpe diem, nothing planned. Clare labored to make it all sound like happenstance, which of course made him the more suspect. He rummaged through the photographs for any that included Christina. But there were none. There was Ben on the sailboat, Ben in the kitchen, Ben and Clare smiling from their places at a table on the porch of what looked like an old hotel. The table was clearly set for two. Where, he wondered, was Christina? Where were Harold and Olive? Where were the photos of the "girl things" they had done? Afraid of the answers, he never asked.

He'd met Ben once, the year they all drove east to visit Harold and Olive in Westchester. Harold was wealthy and worked in the city making investments for an insurance company. All of Harold and Olive's friends were, like them, fifty-ish, well off, fit and always grinning. None of them smoked. They all took vitamins. Everyone observed some New Age regimen to guarantee a particular wellness. Ben was the heroically still married to his disabled wife next-door neighbor and artist who lived on his earnings as an illustrator but was really just waiting to sell his oils. He was tall and smooth skinned and deeply tanned, and his white hair and full beard made him look almost biblical. He'd done some covers for *Life Magazine* and the *Saturday Evening Post.* Clare had confessed to Adrian the crush she'd had on Ben as a girl when, visiting at her uncle's after her parents' divorce, Ben had made a fuss over her in some way she never elaborated, something to do with Rockefeller Center. He would have been in his thirties then and she'd always really "felt really very flattered, you know, that he'd make such a fuss over a fifteen-year-old girl."

Clare's father had left when she was twelve, for reasons that were never made clear to her. One day he came in and said that he would always love her and then he left. Her mother always looked a little wounded after that but never said a word about the divorce except "I'm a one-man woman," which is why, Clare reasoned, her mother never remarried. After that they spent most summers and most Christmases with Uncle Harold and Aunt Olive.

All these years since, it all looked simple and predictable to Adrian now—the girl abandoned by her father as a child looking for an older man's approval, attention, etc., etc., etc.—it was all embarrassingly usual, unremarkable in every way. They had arranged their little off-season tryst while Adrian, the earnest ignoramus, stayed home with the kids and the church work, the reliable garden-variety cuckold and bumpkin.

The *Anna C.* sounded its horn once and made its way out past the harbor's bars and seafood restaurants, out past the sunbathers waving from shore, out past the rock pilings covered with cormorants into the open water, followed by maybe two dozen gulls, which soared alongside the ferry for food tossed from passengers. Adrian Littlefield, seated between strangers on the long bench on the top deck, considered his fellow passengers from the isolation he had learned to wrap around himself in public transit. There were couples with children, college students in packs of various sizes, Asian tourists, and pairs of lovers, some obviously married, some obviously not. He watched as they grew more affectionate the farther out from port the boat traveled. The touching and hugging and holding and even kissing grew more manifest as the mainland grew more distant. This he assigned to the crossing of water, the sense of privacy that passage to an island must add to the sense that all lovers share of being alone against the world and its elements.

When the island came into view, he could see the tall sand cliffs, the green headlands, and the litter of sailing boats. From the dock in Old Harbor, Block Island seemed to Adrian like a postcard of the up-market Yankee resort—huge painted Victorian hotels overlooking the harbor with red, white, and blue buntings hanging from their broad verandas, sloops and schooners and power yachts scattered around the seafront, brightly painted shop fronts done up for the season, and an abundance of cedar shingled housing, graying but not particularly aged. Everywhere there were tanned and happy people in shorts and sandals and designer eyewear, going about no particular business. There were bicycles and mopeds and cars for hire. The dockside was busy with day-trippers and courtesy vans from the various hotels meeting their guests. There were grandparents to welcome their visiting families and the predictable vignettes of arrival and departure that are all the business of ports of call.

Adrian Littlefield waited while the other passengers disembarked. The organizer from the NAFLA group was reminding the attorneys to "be back for the four o'clock ferry back! We have the installation of officers ball tonight at Foxwoods!" This gave the group five hours to tour the island, maybe take a swim, maybe browse the shops for souvenirs. Adrian waited for the rest to leave. He wanted to do his tour alone. He walked up the town, looking over the offerings in store windows, admiring the lithe bodies of women in beachwear, looking into the faces of men. At the top of the main street where the road turned sharply left, he came to the National Hotel. It looked familiar to him. He climbed the front steps and took a seat on the long porch where lunch was being served. He ordered ice tea and, from the list of appetizers, steamers in drawn butter, seafood chowder, crab-cakes, and bruschetta. A little taste of everything, he thought. He had a good view of the harbor and the foot traffic coming and going along the main street front.

There were fathers with cell phones, their teenagers on holidays with their noncustodial parents—subversive daughters being courted by their new stepmothers, young boys bristling at the new men in their mothers' lives. There were young couples traveling *en famille*, with toddlers and infants and bored preteens.

He could see in the faces of the young husbands the fear he had felt in himself at that age, that he'd be overwhelmed at any minute by the duties and expenses and decisions.

He could see in the faces of their wives the worry and regret and second-guessing. How, they seemed to be asking themselves, had they gotten themselves into this predicament? They had been young and footloose and passionate and now they were homebound and bored and fatigued by motherhood and family life. They had been creative and well read and interesting. Now they were dull, bored, vexed by the daylong needs of their offspring.

Adrian tried to reckon the ones who would make it and the ones who wouldn't. He tried to guess, by something in the way they walked or interacted, which of the children for whom this would be the last real family vacation. In the future there would be other configurations of adults and siblings in their lives. Partners, companions, significant others, spousal equivalents, stepparents, stepsisters, half brothers. But for many this would be the last vacation where mother and father shared the same time of their lives.

He was aware of a kind of psychic wince that always registered wrongly as a smile on his face whenever he looked at children and thought of his own children's pain, courageously borne in the years after their mother left. Of course, there was nothing he could do. Still he suffered a kind of survivor's guilt that what had been the best change in his life and the lightning rod of his success had, in ways he sensed but could not measure, hobbled his son and daughter somehow. He had been a good parent and a good provider but he had not loved their mother. And now, in their young adulthood, he could see in the lives of his son and daughter that essential mistrust of their own hearts, a wariness about the love of others that made it difficult for them to form intimate attachments. He looked for early signals of such things in the manner and conduct of the children passing by.

He could see as well the older men eyeing the younger women and felt a quiet kinship with them. Adrian had counted it among the blessings of age that the abundance of women he found attractive was ever broadening even if his sexual prowess began to falter. The older he became, the more younger women there were to look at. Their beauty, at every age, took more of his breath away than it had as a boy.

Of course, he no longer "blamed" Clare for her infidelities. Nor could he much blame Ben for taking advantage of her situation. They were the necessary precipitators or necessary events— an evolution, a natural elaboration of an order whereby the universe of love and attachment purges itself of anomalies. A man of fifty something—as Adrian was now, as Ben was then— could not easily resist the proffered affections of a woman twenty years his junior. Nor could a woman unhappy in her home life, tired of small towns and small children, bored by her husband's regular and routine affections, worried over the pressing and passage of time, be expected to travel in the off-season with a handsome artist to a distant island to sail and walk deserted beaches and talk over dinner, idling away the remains of the day and not offer her body to him. Especially when he had made a fuss over her as a girl. It was only "natural" for a woman at loose ends and a man in his fifties to fall into a fitful consortium should the occasion arise.

Adrian Littlefield had himself made a habit of confirming this in the years since, every chance he got, which was mostly at conventions such as the one he was currently hired to hold forth to. Attended as they always were by more than a few of the recently divorced, or recently traded in for a younger, fresher model, or recently disappointed in love or perennially discontented with life, these professional conferences provided cover for those occasions when the sexually rejected might reconfirm their sexiness. Chief among the obligations—Adrian knew this from his own experience—of every newly divorced man and woman was to demonstrate that it was not a sexual dysfunction that occasioned the breakup. As the keynoter and visiting expert at these confabs and conventions, Adrian was often the focus of much of the free floating, unattached, ready-willing-and-able sexual energy of the registrants, a number of whom, it never failed, would make known in the usual ways to Adrian, their availability for more intimate conversations on related themes. He was possessed, after all, of a certain celebrity in these circles. He was famously single, well spoken, well dressed, well paid and the center of an hour or two hours' attention during which he would motivate, inspire, entertain, inform, and uplift his listeners. This almost always suited his own purposes. He had no less an appetite for a stranger's affections than any man or woman. And while he sometimes missed the predictable lovemaking of the married life, he found it hard to count as anything but good fortune that the eighteen years since the dissolution of his marriage had been characterized by more abundant if more distant, more passionate if less precise, hungrier if less often sated, more memorable if often nameless sexual encounters. If each partner in these arrangements felt equally "used" it was, all the same, a fellow feeling that seemed to him and to no few of the women he had had sex with, enough. That bodies could pleasure and could be pleasured, free of social, emotional, or intellectual encumbrances, seemed to Adrian a good and wholesome thing. And he made it his mission to attend to his partner in ways that would overwhelm whatever residual regret she might otherwise attach to the "one-night stand." With several of these women he had maintained an ongoing correspondence, some of which had ended sooner, some later, and some remained pleasant and unpredictable addendums to his professional life. Sometimes he would invite one of them to join him on an extended speaking tour. They would spend a week—sometimes two—together.

They'd begin to behave like real companions. He'd remember how she drank her coffee and order room service accordingly. She'd pack and unpack his things between hotels. They would tell each other secrets over dinner. It warmed something in Adrian he could never quite identify. Getting to know someone after he had gotten to have sex with them was a reversal of the usual arrangement by which the business of intimacy was in the main conducted, but for a variety of reasons, it appealed to him. The flesh, Adrian sometimes pointed out in his workshops, is far less particular than the heart or the mind, when it came to finding "suitable" partners. Sex between people who might not otherwise find anything to admire about one another could be quite, well, satisfactory, especially on a time-fixed basis. Whereas, he would likewise observe, there were people who could be attracted in every possible way, intimate in all ways in the conduct of their lives together, but sexually uninspired. These were but a few among the many mysteries his programs dealt with. And Adrian had seen in the faces of the registrants at Foxwoods, in the small talk of the NAFLA conferees, in the body language of their pairings and couplings and comminglings at the welcome reception the night before, chit-chatting with wines and finger-foods, the men in their best business-casual attire, the women wanting to look professional but sexy—he had seen it all—the whole register of human want and willingness and desire.

Adrian could see it now, watching from the long porch of the National Hotel, the parade of suffering humankind, bearing their various histories and fears of missed chances and discontents along the esplanade, the mercilessly sunlit day unfolding around them: it was inevitable. "The story of love," as he often told his audience, "to quote Professor Bowlby, is told in three volumes: Attachment, Separation and Loss." Or if the time allowed only a thumbnail version, "Love," he'd say, quoting Roy Orbison, "hurts."

He finished his meal, left a large gratuity, and asked the waitress for a local phone book.

In the directory he looked for Ben Walters. There was only one, on Pilot Hill Road. He looked at the map. It was a little ways southwest of town. He went down to the taxi ranks near the boat docks and climbed in an old station wagon, "Island Hack & Taxi Tours" painted on its doors.

"Tour of the island?" the old woman at the wheel asked him.

"How long does it take?" he asked.

"How long do you have?"

"I have to be back for the four o'clock ferry."

"No problem," she told him. "That's acres of time. It really is a tiny island."

Adrian got in and introduced himself.

"Adrian Littlefield." He extended his hand.

"Gloria, Gloria Dodge," she said. "You're welcome to the island. First time here?"

"Yes, well . . . yes, my first time."

She drove out of the parking lot and turned northwards going out past the hotels, the local bars, the long beaches packed with sunbathers. Adrian kept a map and watched the sights and signposts go by. Gloria kept up the travelogue.

"The island is only seven miles long by three miles wide, shaped like a pork chop, less than eleven square miles." Gloria had this "tour" memorized. Adrian looked at the fold-up map of the island he'd been given by the tour organizers. Block Island did, indeed, look like a pork chop with the narrow bony end to the north and the squat round meaty end to the south. There was a profusion of dune and seascape as they drove out of town.

"That's Scotch Beach there, a little rougher water. It was named for the people who didn't want to pay the dime a week to help with the upkeep of the beaches. They could swim there free."

Adrian smiled and nodded and feigned interest. The old station wagon bumped along out what he read was Corn Neck Road past Bush Lot Hill toward Chaqum Pond at the north end of the island.

"Many people live here year round?" he asked.

"I guess they figure around nine hundred now. Most of these homes are seasonals. People from Providence and Hartford and Boston and New York. Many of the same families are coming for generations. I've been here my entire life. We raised seven children here. Seventeen grandchildren and nine great-grandchildren. They'll all be coming home next week. My husband's birthday."

"Wow," said Adrian and looked out at the sea.

At the end of the road was a rock beach, a small parking lot, and off to the west an old lighthouse.

"Eighteen sixty-seven it was built. They're making it into a museum. My son is on the volunteer committee. If you want to get out and have a look I'll wait."

Adrian shook his head and she backed the car around to head back on the road they'd come.

"How old will your husband be?"

"Well, he'd have been eighty but he died last year. Still, we figured we'd get together anyway, and celebrate, you know . . . it's all just family."

"That must be very hard," said Adrian, a little worried that he'd gotten more information about Gloria than he ever wanted but figuring now there was no turning back.

"Well, of course, we all miss him terribly. He was the dearest man and the grandchildren were so sad, so beautiful . . . they wanted to have a cake and get out all the pictures. I can't wait to see them. They're coming from as far away as Denver. He was the dearest man, everybody's favorite. He always loved it when they came to visit us here on the island."

"Won't that be nice?" Adrian said. "Look at those beautiful yachts!"

They'd come to the marina at the Great Salt Pond and the New Harbor area. Sailboats tied to their moorings rocked in the wide basin. Fashionably clad boaters walked up and down the docks. A restaurant called Dead Eye Dicks was doing a brisk luncheon trade. The old wagon passed a small graveyard on the left.

"He's buried in there," said Gloria.

Adrian said nothing, hoping the conversation might take another turn.

"Fifty-eight years we were married. But we'd been 'together' for years before that. I met him when I was thirteen. It was February. I was ice-skating with friends and all they could do was laugh at me because I kept falling and I couldn't stand up. The legs would go right out from under me. They were all laughing. It was horrible. And all of a sudden, I look up and this boy is holding out a hockey stick to me. 'Grab on,' he says to me, 'I'll pull you to shore.' And after he had rescued me, he sat me on a bench on the shore and knelt and untied my skates and helped me on with my boots and I thought, what a beautiful boy, what a beautiful boy."

"You were very young," Adrian said. The car turned south on the West Side Road.

"Well, it was three years later. I was sixteen. I was walking into town and he stopped his truck and asked if I wanted a lift. And at first I said, 'No thanks,' because I didn't want to be too easy but he just leaned over and said, 'Are you sure?' and I thought, well, why not? I climbed in and we've been together ever since. The day they bombed Pearl Harbor he asked me to marry him. He knelt down just the way he had when he rescued me that time, you know, to untie my skates, only this time he asked me to marry him. And I thought what a beautiful man he is. We had the wedding on New Year's Eve. It was 1941. He left for the Navy three days later. He was a UDT man. Well, you know, growing up on the island, he knew how to swim. I was nineteen. He was twenty."

Adrian looked at the weathered old woman beside him and tried to imagine her at nineteen. He tried to imagine what it took to marry a man and sleep with a man who was leaving for war and might never return. He wondered if she had been faithful to him. He wondered if he had been faithful to her. He wondered if they discussed such things in those days.

"What was his name?" Adrian asked her.

"Bob. Well, Robert. Well, Bob . . . Bob Dodge." Her eyes were red and watering now. There was no sadness in her voice. Only resignation. But her eyes were brimming with real tears. They'd nearly made it to the southeast corner of the island.

Gloria pulled into a parking area below another lighthouse.

"Take a walk out there and you'll be able to see the end of Long Island," she said, "and Mohegan Bluffs and the Southeast Lighthouse. They had to move the thing back a few years ago. It would have fallen into the sea. And you can say you stood in Rhode Island and saw New York."

Adrian had no interest in the lighthouse or Long Island or a walk in the sand but he figured Gloria might want a moment to compose herself. So he took the path out among the scrub trees and Rosa Ragosa shrubs to where a wooden deck overlooked the high bluffs and the beach below. He stood and looked at the seascape, killing what he figured was enough time for Gloria to get herself together, and then walked back to the car where she was finishing a cigarette.

"Great view isn't it!"

"Yes, yes it is, spectacular."

They got back into the car; Gloria started the engine and backed out the drive. The car worked its way north now, returning to the town of New Shoreham near the Old Harbor. There were still two hours before the return ferry.

"Do you know Pilot Hill Road?" Adrian asked. "Do you know someone by the name of Ben Walters?"

"There was a Walters up that way, all right. Just above Tug Hole. His wife was sick in some way. I think she died. Summer people from New York. He painted. You know, pictures. I don't know if he still comes or not. Do you want to go by there? How do you know them?"

"Friend of the family," Adrian said. "If you've got the time, I'd like to have a look."

He didn't know exactly what he wanted to find. He'd never really sorted out his thoughts on the matter. He didn't know what he was supposed to feel or think about it. Ben Walters had only been the first of the infidelities he was sure of. He remembered a time when he hated the name and the idea of another man touching his wife in that way. He'd tried to outgrow those primitive feelings. He could remember, as a much younger man, wishing for the kind of marriage Gloria had had—those long years, those children and grandchildren and great grandchildren, that love and grief and routine. Adrian could remember the times as a young family man driving through small towns in Ohio with Clare on a Sunday afternoon, looking into the tall windows of turn-of-the-century homes with their gingerbread and clapboard and backyard gardens, trying to imagine the orderly good-old-days lives of the inhabitants of such places, where everyone had a huge front porch on which they sat in the evening, drinking lemonade and telling stories and waving at the neighbors who'd be walking by. He could remember how he awoke one morning to find he had that very thing, a settled life in Findlay, Ohio, in an old house with a wide porch and wooden floors and knick-knacks and radiators and a wife whose un-happiness seemed to grow in direct proportion to his happi-ness. He'd wanted that life, the settled, Sunday dinner with the family Rockwell print of an existence in which he'd eventually be the senior pastor of a thriving church where everyone knew everyone and everyone's business and kept an eye out for each other's children and were determined to live happily ever after.

At about the same time, Clare was getting tired of all of that. She wanted to know if he'd consider moving to New York. He could maybe manage one of her Uncle Harold's companies. They could live in Westchester. There would be more money, she was sure. He could commute to the city by train like Uncle Harold did to his office in midtown. She could do photography or videos or something artistic and the kids could get a nanny or go to a fash-ionable day care center and then to a Montessori school. She could come into the city on Friday nights for the theatre; they could ice-skate at the rink at Rockefeller Center as she had done as a girl visi-ting Uncle Harold after her mother and father divorced. They would have interesting friends, an interesting life. She was tired of Ohio and Findlay and the First Methodist Church. She didn't want to be a senior pastor's wife. She didn't want a summer place on Lake Erie. She didn't want to grow old in an old house in the Midwest with a man who was going nowhere.

He told her he thought there were no geographic cures. "Unhappiness," he told her, in the way she hated that ministers had of speaking in slogans, "is portable."

Gloria had turned up High Street and onto a dirt road at Pilot Hill, where she braked suddenly at the entrance to a small two-track drive on the right.

"I think that's the Walters place up there. Go ahead, I'll wait. Take your time."

Adrian hadn't a clue what he was supposed to do, or what it was he wanted to find. What if Ben Walters was there and knew who he was? Maybe he'd read one of his books, or seen him on *Oprah,* or heard him on the radio and knew the connections. What if he didn't know Adrian's connections to the woman he had seduced here almost twenty years ago and how it changed all their lives and left his children motherless and him with his hands full of duty and detail? What if he was only a withered old man walking around in tennis shorts and sandals with leathery skin and a bald head? What if he was senile at seventy something or disabled in some way, or what if he wasn't? What would they have to say to each other?

Adrian could feel his heart racing as he worked his way up

the little gravel drive to the clearing in the woods where a little cedar-shingled cottage appeared surrounded by a little lawn with a few old Adirondack chairs in a semicircle and badly in need of paint. The place was tiny, a story and a half with a screened porch inside of which was what looked like the main door. There was no sign of life anywhere around the place. No car, no open windows, the grass a little overgrown. He tried the screen door, walked in, and knocked at the main door, listening hard for the sound of any movement inside. There was none. He tried the doorknob but it was locked.

There was nothing. Only the sound of catbirds in the thick woods around the place, and the smell of the sea, and the movement of the breeze in the greeny things around the place. There was as well the small noise of a wind chime hanging from a hawthorn tree in the yard, and at a distance, as he listened, the noise of children down the hill near what he guessed was the freshwater pond at the base of the hill. Adrian looked in the window. The interior was small and dark. A table at one end of the kitchen. A fieldstone fireplace at one end of the main room, and a small hallway leading to what must be the bedroom, or bedrooms—maybe two. There were no signs of recent life inside the house.

Adrian walked around to the bedroom window. Through the sheer curtains he could see an old metal bed, a bureau and a chair. Off to one side was a sink and a mirror. The bed was made. There was no disorder to the room.

He looked out across the yard. There was a small shed with windows and a small porch. It was, he reckoned, the artist's studio. He looked inside and saw an easel and a table and jars full of brushes and rags hung from hooks on the wall. No canvases or works in progress were anywhere to be seen.

Adrian walked back across the yard and sat in one of the Adirondack chairs and propped his elbows on the wide arms and rested his chin on his folded hands and wondered what to make of the place. *Surely*, he thought, *Ben Walters would be here in midsummer if he was going to be here at all.* The place's vacancy had about it a permanence that was, to Adrian, palpable. He figured that Ben Walters, now nearing seventy-five, widowed and alone, his little artistic career having come to nothing, must be summering out in assisted living or a nursing home after the second or third stroke had left him paralyzed or dumbstruck. Or maybe he'd lost a leg to diabetes or had bypass surgery or a lung removed. Or maybe he had Alzheimer's and didn't know one day from the next or his last name or who the President of the United States was. Or maybe he was dead, and the deserted house a portion of his estate that would have to be settled. Anyway, Adrian was sure, he was never going to be making the trip or walking the beach or sweeping anyone else's wife off her feet, not in this life, and likely not in another. Ben Walters was no longer a man he need contend with. It was good that he came here to make this clear.

Adrian tried to imagine how it must have been for Clare. Getting her friend Christine to cover for her, getting here, getting it on with the old fart, the romance of it all, the distance from Findlay, Ohio, the hopes for a new, more exciting life.

She'd gotten as far as Cleveland in the years since. She'd married again and divorced again, and again and again. She seemed, these long years since, every bit as discontented, only older. The children had each spent hours with counselors, learning to love their mother without having to approve of her "inappropriate choices," and to maintain the proper "emotional borders" between themselves and their mother's chaotic life.

It occurred to Adrian that if she outlived him, much of his hard-earned estate would work its way to her, through the generosity of his children, who would surely use a portion of their inheritance to support their mother, who could be counted on to be, as ever, in need.

"Oh well," is what he told himself, when such things came to him.

There was nothing about this place, his coming here, that had the sense of portent he had imagined when he first made arrangements to come here. He had simply married the wrong woman. He had chosen wrongly. He had mistaken good sex, hardly a difficult thing at twenty-something, for true affection. He knew it early in the marriage. He remembered the mornings he would awake beside her, knowing that there was nothing about her that he really treasured, really admired, really needed. She was not, he knew, a great mother, an exceptional human, or a particularly good woman. They had had good sex, made good babies, not brought out the worst in each other. But neither had they brought out the best. And he had been, stupidly, willing to live with the consequences of his poor decisions, to tolerate waking next to a woman whom he did not admire in trade for lovely children and an ordinary life free of the larger vexations. He had not, in his marriage to her, abused her physically or verbally. He had tried his very best to make her happy. He hadn't drunk or gambled or cavorted with other women. He'd done his share of diapers and dishes. He had tried to support her efforts to find more interesting things to "do" than "wife and mothering." He had been, in all ways he thought, the reliable husband, the hedged bet against hunger and loneliness, the other body in the bed. He had not, he knew it now, ever loved her. Sitting in the Adirondack chair on Ben Walter's deserted front lawn, Adrian wondered if she'd ever known how much he really didn't love her. Maybe something in her sensed that emptiness and railed against his willingness to live in a loveless if otherwise functional marriage. Maybe it was this that drove her to do what she had done. He had been willing to settle for too little. For her, enough would never be enough. Which aberration of desire, he now wondered, offended God or Nature or the Fates the most.

He walked back to the car where Gloria was just finishing a cigarette. She pressed it out in the ashtray and started the engine.

"Anyone home?"

"No one, nothing there."

"Too bad," she said. "You've come all this way."

"Oh well," Adrian said, "another time maybe."

She backed out to Pilot Hill Road and drove Adrian back to the ferry docks. He gave her a fifty-dollar bill and thanked her for the tour.

"But it's only thirty dollars."

"Buy a little cheer for the birthday party."

"That's really good of you," Gloria said, folding the crisp note into her shirt pocket.

"May I ask you," Adrian said, leaning back with one foot out of the car, "may I ask you, Gloria, did you ever find yourself, like ever, in those fifty-eight years, you know, married to Bob, did you ever wonder 'what the hell am I doing here?' You know, with the kids and the work and the routine?"

"No," she said without hesitation, "never once. I was just so glad to have him home, safe, after the war, I'd missed him so. And I thought, I always thought, what a beautiful man, what a good man he was. So I can tell you, we had our hard days, sure. But no, I never wondered about being with him. I wish I were with him now. I can still feel him."

There was a catch in her breath. Her hands dropped from the steering wheel of the old wagon. Adrian said nothing.

"The young these days are so unhappy, so impatient, so full of expectations. All we wanted was to survive it. To be together. To get through, Bob and me, you know, and for the children . . . Nowadays they just want too much. Whatever they have, they think there must be more. They want so much they don't know what they want."

50

She was staring at a point in the middle of the steering wheel. She caught her breath again.

"Yes, yes, I suppose that's it."

Adrian wondered what it was he wanted. He had long since lost hope of a woman who could love him like a wife would and love his children like a mother. That mix of passion and sacrifice seemed quite impossible to him now. Not because such women did not exist, but because he lacked what it was they wanted. Though he had housekeepers and nannies and tutors and teachers and therapists for his children, though he could find a woman any night of the week to pleasure and who would pleasure him, there had not been nor would there be, he now knew with certainty, anyone like Gloria in his life and times—a woman who would mourn and remember the boy he had been, the man he was, the old man he hoped to be, who would love him and outlive him and keep him alive in the daily lives and times of his people, his children and his children's children. He could feel the wave of sadness rising in him that he knew, if he did not move, would overtake him.

He closed the car door and made for the ferry.

"Safe home!" she shouted after him.

Boarding the boat, Adrian blew kisses.

THOMAS LYNCH is a writer and funeral director. His collections of poems include *Skating with Heather Grace, Grimalkin & Other Poems,* and *Still Life in Milford. The Undertaking,* his first book of nonfiction, won The American Book Award and was a finalist for the National Book Award; *Bodies in Motion and at Rest* won the Great Lakes Book Award, and *Booking Passage* was named a 2006 Notable Book by the Library of Michigan. A book of short stories, *Late Fictions,* will be published in 2008. He lives in Milford, Michigan, where he has been a funeral director since 1974, and in Moveen, Co. Clare, Ireland, where he keeps an ancestral cottage.

Isaac Laquedem

By Kevin Macnish

*It is the elegance of the telling of this tale that first
strikes the reader: "Isaac Laquedem" reads like a story
that has existed for years in a library much like the
one in which the narrator here finds himself. But
upon closer inspection, it is its exploration of the myth
of the Wandering Jew, and the matters of humility
and faith, that magnifies the artistry of the sentences.*

—BRET LOTT

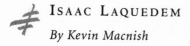

ISAAC LAQUEDEM

By Kevin Macnish

I had been staying at the Palazzo Casubaldo for a little under a week, a guest of the Marquesa with whose son I had been at university. Events had transpired so that my friend was unable to join me when I arrived, and so I found myself committed to spending an indeterminate time alone in Florence. Although known better for their wine than their erudition, the Casubaldo family has an unusual library, thanks largely to Pierro, a wayward son who in the mid-nineteenth century decided to concentrate on collecting medieval manuscripts rather than improving the soil of their vineyards. The result was a temporary setback in the quality of their wine and the size of their income, but an impressively eclectic library. Hence I took to diverting myself in this dusty, unfrequented room while I waited for my friend to arrive.

The library is in a terrible state, the opprobrium received by Pierro having deterred others from since having much to do with it. The cataloguing accords to his own unique system, the explanation for which no longer survives if indeed it was ever written. It is also compiled entirely in his own hand, which is no paragon of clarity. Given that I was not searching for anything in particular, other than a means to kill time, I had therefore taken to perusing the shelves at random and taking down a book for the day in the hope that it may throw out something interesting. It was with this idle interest, then, that I discovered a copy of Leonard Doldius's *Praxis Alchymiae*, written in Nürnberg at the turn of the seventeenth century in response to the bizarre claims of Paracelsus.

I had not progressed very far when I allowed my eye to be distracted by a curious man in the street below. He appeared to be in conversation with Graziano, the Sardinian *portiere* of the palazzo, but it was his dress and manner that particularly caught my attention. A tall man with long hair, I would imagine that he was aged somewhere between fifty and seventy years. His clothes were tattered and he wore no shoes, but had a purple coat which reached to his feet. In this respect, he differed little from any unfortunate to walk the streets of Florence, but there was a diffidence in his manner and a pallor in his cheek that were in contrast to those others. He was clearly not asking for money, as I had seen Graziano deal tersely with such before now.

Not finding the *Praxis Alchymiae* to hold much of interest beyond a note by the Latin translator regarding a story that Paracelsus was not in fact dead but merely sleeping in his tomb in Strasburg thanks to his own libations, I determined to pursue the man in the hope of finding better company than the physician of Nürnberg.

By the time I had left the library and caught up with Graziano the man had gone. Nonetheless, he was able to indicate the direction in which my quarry had gone, and so, having asked a number of others, I came to the Piazza Santo Spirito. Here I found him washing his face in the fountain, looking at first glance to be just another of the derelicts that inhabit the square. With some caution I approached him and asked if he had eaten that day. He replied in the negative and, with some cajoling, he agreed to join me for a beer and a *panino* on one of the benches surrounding the fountain.

He did not eat as a man starving, nor even missing his food, as his wasted figure had led me to imagine. Rather he took small bites which he chewed on methodically, interrupted with similarly small quantities of beer. As we talked, he gave his name as Isaac, a Jew from the Holy City, who had been walking the streets of Europe for some time. He had a sound knowledge of his hometown, tracing some of the developments there over the last few hundred years, although he admitted that he had not been back since he was about forty years of age. Our conversation then turned to Florence, and particularly the square in which we sat, dominated by the Chiesa Santo Spirito, the last to be built by Brunelleschi and at one time a large Augustinian monastery where Michelangelo had dissected corpses in search of the human form.

Isaac talked intimately of Michelangelo and the Italian Renaissance, from which it sometimes feels as if the city is yet to escape. He struck me as a man of learning who must have fallen on hard times, although to judge from his appearance he must have spent the best part of the last twenty years living on the streets. I pressed him on his life story, on how he came to his current position, and still wonder about his response.

He claimed to have been born in Jerusalem a century and a half after the Maccabee had freed his people from the abomination of desolation. When he was of age he worked with his father, a cobbler, making sandals in the city. At his father's death, Isaac took over the business along with a lucrative relationship with the local Roman garrison for military footwear. A good Jew, he would attend the Temple regularly and, living in Jerusalem, was able to attend the three annual festivals required of all men while his business benefited from the simultaneous influx of visitors to the city.

Not long after he had assumed the running of the business, talk in the city had turned to the existence of a new claimant to the title of Messiah from Nazareth. Although this was more likely a pretender such as Theudas or Judas of Galilee, nonetheless Isaac found himself torn between his business with the Romans and his desire to see the nations flock to Jerusalem as the true center of the world, as spoken of by the prophets. He determined to hear this man when next he came to the city.

He did not have long to wait: shortly before the Passover

feast this teacher arrived in the city. He entered on a donkey in fulfilment of prophecy and making no uncertain claim to his kingship. The people had rushed to the streets to welcome him waving palm branches, the sign of the Maccabees. Over the coming days, the Nazarene had made bold statements regarding the destruction of Jerusalem, of the Temple itself, and of the end of times when Yahweh would restore all to its rightful place. Isaac had become caught up in the excitement and cheered when he heard that his generation would not pass away before these things were to occur.

Two days later the Nazarene was arrested, tried, and found guilty of sedition, ordered to die on a cross. Broken with disappointment, the cobbler had stood in his doorway to watch the condemned man pass on his way to Golgotha. As he passed the house, streaked with blood after a severe whipping, the pretender had collapsed on the doorstep. Unable to restrain his anger and resentment, Isaac kicked him and spat on him, this false messiah who had lasted less than a week in the city. As the teacher looked up at him, Isaac hissed, "I believed in you. I wanted to see the things you promised, but your words were empty and your promises shallow. I despise you." A member of the crowd came forward to help the unfortunate with the crossbeam from which he was to hang, and as he rose to his feet he looked with sadness at the cobbler and replied, "See them you shall. You shall know me better in those days."

Confused, the cobbler felt compelled to follow the crowd

up to the place of the skull and watch the nails driven home. He had joined with the taunts at first, but half-heartedly, and eventually stopped altogether. He found that there was something terribly sad in the man on the cross which the crowd did not appear to see, except for the small band of women and a young man wailing loudly. That night he went to his bed troubled.

A week later, he heard the new rumours that the Nazarene was risen from the dead and had been seen in the city. His heart stopped. Was this true? Had he really cheated the grave? His questions were answered the following week when a stranger came to the table where he worked in front of the house. Not recognizing him at first, he was asking whether the stranger wanted new or repairs when the words caught in his throat. He saw a simple scar on the wrist of the man as he reached out to pick up a sandal. At this, the stranger looked at him directly. "Isaac," he said, "I have called you by name. You are mine. I will have need of you yet, and you shall see the city that I promised." Distraught at his wickedness, the cobbler turned and fled.

At first he had traveled to Antioch. It was here that he met the Pharisee Saul who had himself seen the risen Messiah and enjoyed fellowship with the growing body of believers, although always feeling himself an outsider. Here also was he baptized by Ananias, changing his name to Joseph. With time he moved to Babylon, and then to Alexandria, where he spent his time in the library and heard of the destruction of Herod's temple. A short while later, he was in Rome when Nero set it ablaze. He traveled frequently to avoid the persecutions that were to befall many of his new family, and confined himself to the coastal areas of northern Africa. Following the Edict of Milan he journeyed to that city, studying under the bishop Jerome.

The man claimed to have traveled extensively in the East, knowing the father of Mohammed when he dwelt at Ormuz and witnessing the death of Christ to the prophet himself. He recalled conversations with an Archbishop in Armenia as well as other eastern prelates. He had conversed with Fadhilah after the capture of Elvan and claimed to have been intimately familiar with many of the crusaders and their Arab enemies. Later he traveled north to Poland, Moscow, Sweden, and Denmark. At Hamburg he had met Paul von Eitzen, who was to become Bishop of Schleswig, and in Madrid Secretary Christopher Krause, then legate to the Court of Spain. Having spent so many years traveling he found it impossible to settle, and continued to traverse Europe and the near East, although he never had the courage to return to his home city.

Isaac stopped then, seeming to tire. I offered Isaac more food, but he would take none, claiming that he received his sustenance from the Lord. I managed to prevail upon him to take some money, which he did albeit under protest. With that he craved my indulgence and took his leave to attend the offices in San Marco, on the north side of the Arno. I followed him for a few minutes, long enough to see him give my money to a gypsy

on the steps of Chiesa Santo Spirito, and then I returned to the
house of the Casubaldos.

What did I make of his strange story? Somehow I could not
put it down to a lie. The man was too compelling, and his manner unlike that of any liar that I have met. Besides which, to what
end would he profit in spending an hour of his time telling me a
fantastic story and then refusing food or money for the road,
both of which I judged he was in need? My feeling was that he at
least was convinced of his tale. Yet while I am no physician, still
less versed in the vagaries of the human mind, nor could I con-
clude that he was mad. Indeed I have scarcely met a man more
sober, aside from his bizarre claim to longevity. Any further
alternatives I can only leave to the reader to determine. I shall
myself always remember him as the cobbler from Jerusalem.

KEVIN MACNISH is half-Scottish, half-Welsh and grew up moving around Europe, living in England, Cyprus, Germany, and Denmark. He has a degree in philosophy from universities in England (Leeds) and Denmark (Aarhus) and has earned a master's degree in apologetics from Southern Evangelical Seminary, North Carolina, and another in international relations from the University of East Anglia, England. He currently lives in Rome, Italy, where he teaches philosophy and apologetics in a Christian arts center with his wife, Barbara, and their two children, Christopher and Helena.

The Train to Ghent

by A. H. Wald

"The Train to Ghent" is a love story, plain and simple. But what makes it transcend that summary assessment is the story of Joseph's innocence in the face of age-old superstition, and his willingness to step out in the childlike faith all of us must take, in order to find that path toward love.

—Bret Lott

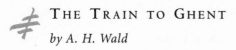

THE TRAIN TO GHENT
by A. H. Wald

"How did you end up in Ghent?" Monique asked.

Joseph watched her hand wave like a handkerchief through the smoke circling around the cramped café and then pointed to her coffee saucer. "Could I have that sugar if you're not going to use it?"

"You can't tell me? What is it, some big secret?" she asked as she pushed the packet across the table.

Joseph smiled. He liked how curious she was about everything, what he ate, where he slept, how he cut his hair, how he survived the winter cold. When they first met, he had been wary, afraid she might be mocking him like his brothers who had harassed him for his toys and laughed at his odd piggish face and told him he was too ugly to come from their tribe. Their questions still taunted him in his head, "Why are you squinting at that book, Joseph? What are you dreaming about now, old man?"

But Monique fascinated him too much for him to remain

self-conscious with her. In her monochrome clothes the color of earth and stone, she was a reverse image of the women he had grown up with. Skin as white as his was black, so pale he could see the bluish veins crisscrossing on her wrists, stringy hair like straw, and instead of taut, ebony skin stretched over high smooth bones, her face caved in on itself with barely a chin or a jaw, just thin lips that looked like rind without any juice left, and doughy cheeks that sagged a little like dumplings. Yet even though she was not beautiful, she was a marvel to him: the way she focused her attention on a difficult problem, and asked the professor a razor-sharp question that no one else was smart enough to ask. And outside of class, she spoke with an awkward nervousness he had known before only in himself.

He tore the corner off the packet and twirled the triangle into a tight white thread. "A train brought me."

"All the way from Africa?" She shook her head skeptically; the flat ends of her hair flared out in a circle.

He frowned at her and then turned to look out the window to the row of gray apartments across the wet street. They had known each other how long? Five, six weeks since the winter term had started, and had talked in lab twice, and she still could not speak the name of his country; he was only a continent to her. He wanted her to say, "All the way from Ghana? All the way from Bimbilla?" When he had written to his mother, he told her, "I have met Monique Julien, from Antwerp, Belgium." Not "a fellow engineering student," or "my future girlfriend," or "the woman I will ask to be my wife"—a wild prediction formed one night when he could not sleep and he dreamed of the two of them walking with their coffee-colored children around the lip of the fountain in the square.

"On a train?" she echoed like a child, a habit he could see might irritate him someday.

"A train," he said firmly, hoping she would leave it at that. The frayed cuff of his long underwear wormed out of his shirt sleeve as he slowly stirred the sugar in his coffee, and then he brought his other hand over the warm drift of steam rising from the cup. A dull song began to throb out of the café speakers and suddenly he missed the beat of the music back home, drumming in his blood.

"You just hopped on a train and it brought you all the way here, over the sea?"

"No, not that kind of train," he said. He looked out at the apartment block and saw irregular ovals of dampness staining the façade like dark clouds on the paler stone, and along the bottom, a line of leafless saplings growing in the concrete side-walk, each with its own perfect circle of dirt. A bus sprayed through the remains of the morning drizzle and blotted out the street. Joseph caught a glimpse of a familiar advertisement on the bus, a picture of a group of suited businessmen, briefcases in hand, stepping onto the Eurostar to cross the channel. Somehow he had to make Monique understand who he was, how he had been transported here to this moment and this place. Not Joseph from Africa, but Joseph Solanga from Bimbilla, Ghana, the last runty son of the family, his mother's pet and only hope after the six other sons had squirmed free of her missionary school dreams.

He saw himself again as a studious, unsmiling boy with a big pea-shaped head filled with diagrams and sketches on another sullen day. But it had been hot and muggy with the moisture sagging in the air, thick enough to hold the spiders Ezra claimed could cross the yard without a web. Ghost spiders Moses called them, trying to frighten Joseph. He remembered how stiff and scratchy his new shirt was that his mother had made from a piece of bright blue andikra cloth. He wanted to wear his softer threadbare hand-me-down shirt but his mother insisted, and when his brothers saw it, they threatened to sell him to the slave traders that supposedly still worked the river. He could not tell if they were joking or not, and on the long walk to the main road in the village, he did not dare leave his mother's side. The yellow-white pupil of the sun stared down at them, beaming heat into the afternoon air, and Joseph wished his father had not been away working in the mines so he could have ridden on his shoulders.

By the time they reached the road, most of the village was already waiting to see Mr. Sarbah's coffin go by. There was not a stir of wind, except for the drafts the older women made fanning themselves with wing-flapped hands. Then cotton plumes began to mass above the savannah, and worried murmurs passed down the line that a downpour might ruin the parade. The stories were carried along too; how Fatu Dendo, the best carver in the region, had charged triple his usual fee, and how sick Mr. Sarbah had been before he had recovered, and how the coffin would have to be displayed in the front yard because it was too wide to fit through the double front doors and too long for the covered porch.

Joseph remained next to his mother in a patch of women, and fiddled with the truck he had made out of two Fanta bottle caps and a bit of wire, while the other children played jokes with each other and scuffed up the red powdered dirt. Samuel and Zebulon came back to pester him for the truck. "Come on, old man," they teased him with the nickname he hated. But Joseph pretended he had left the truck at home and would not move from his protected spot, shielded in the drape of his mother's skirt. Samuel came back again. "Come on, I know you have it." He kept his eyes on Joseph, hoping to see a flicker of admission.

"No I don't, leave me alone." He could feel his breath turning shallow, and tried to take a gulp of air.

Samuel gave him a soft punch on the arm. "Next time, I'll hit you harder."

"Make your own truck," Joseph said.

"It's bad luck to bring a truck to the parade. Mr. Sarbah's death is going to come to you instead."

"I told you, I left it at home." The drums were pounding in the distance, signaling that the coffin was on its way, and he knew if he could just hold on a little bit longer, Samuel would get distracted.

"Hand it over or else I'll come back with Ezra and Isaac to hold you down," Samuel whispered in his ear, pressing his knuckles on Joseph's hip bone. "If you cry, I'll make sure you don't eat for a week."

Joseph debated through the pain. He could easily make another truck, but it wasn't right for Samuel to take what wasn't his. "Stop it," he hissed back.

"Come on, give it to me," Samuel said, making his tone sound friendly. "I won't bother you anymore. I promise."

Joseph pushed closer into his mother, and her palm stroked the fuzz on his head with a preoccupied attention. Then the booming beat of the drummers became louder, pulsing and pounding through the air, and in a predictable flash, Samuel turned to follow the noise. His mother craned her long neck and announced that the coffin was coming. Joseph released his grasp from the metal scoring his palm and slipped the truck into his pocket with a deep breath. Then the crowd started to squeeze in around him, and he fought for his footing in the throbbing current of the line. But his mother knotted her hand around his fist like the end of a rope, and with a small bounce of her arm she tested the snugness of the bond.

The pungent scent of a sweat-drenched shirt rubbed past his cheek, and he caught sight of two toga-clad elders tapping their gold-tipped staffs ahead of them, and a crescendo of praise fluttered up from the crowd, "Oh yes, oh my, yes he did it, can you believe it, look at that, oh what a sight." Joseph saw on the other side of the road, the older men roll their shoulders and the young men begin to strut dance steps in their row. The women started to sway and raise their arms, and the throng pressed so tight that for a moment he thought he would be kneaded and folded into the mass of clammy flesh. Then he was squirted out like a fish escaping from a pair of hands, first his head, then his skinny chest and legs, and then his mother's hand let his arm go free in the crush, and he stumbled into the road. He stood stunned at the shiny disc coming toward him.

"Get out of the way," a servant hauling a rope yelled to him.

Joseph stared at the face of a train gleaming in the sun, shimmering in its glossy skin of paint, the bell clanging, the towering steam pipe, the glint of the flanged grill supporting the engine nose that chugged along with the groans of servants who pulled the wagon underneath it.

"Watch out, boy!"

He stood bolted in place. The only impulse he felt was to lift up his arms and embrace the amazing coffin that had been birthed from the mind of Fatu Dendo. Around him, the villagers swarmed into the road toward the train like bees to a queen, swelling up and then quickly falling back, careful not to touch the coffin and die. But Joseph did not care. The coffin train bore down, but still he did not move. He opened his eyes as wide as they would go, bunching up the skin on his forehead. He wanted his eyes to take over his face and merge into one big eye to capture this vision and bring it into his own mind in one simple gulp like a snake swallowing a monkey. Then someone jerked him back to the line.

His mother's hand sought his again and squeezed it with her own burst of pleasure. Slow flies lit on his lips and forehead but he was afraid to brush them off and miss a precious second of the train growing bigger and grander in front of him, like banana leaves unfurling in the rainy season, a magical instantaneous growth, except this wasn't a living creature. It was the vision of a man manufactured into length and height and volume, and the thought made Joseph's jaw go slack. The objects Joseph dreamed in his head were no larger than the palm of his hand; he had not imagined it possible to contain something as huge as a real car or a bus in his head. But Fatu Dendo, so old and hobbled that his skin was shrinking on his skull, had managed to conceive of something so much bigger than himself, and then, in a greater miracle, translated it into the squares and rectangles and circles and joined them together with rods and bars. Joseph watched as the long rectangle of one car went by and then another, and then another with windowed sides and painted gold curlicues coiling on the emerald green frame.

At the end came the neat square of a maroon caboose, but no one wanted to give up their place alongside the coffin train, and the crowd shambled along.

"All aboard," Moses shouted with a mischievous smile as he

walked down the line. A nervous laugh went up from the crowd. "All aboard," Moses shouted again, looking at Joseph and daring him with a nod.

Joseph didn't need any more encouragement. He wriggled his fingers to free them from his mother's hand. She adjusted her grip, he wriggled more insistently. If she had not released him, he would have torn his fingers off, but she opened her hand and he slipped out, his legs pumping up and down like the pistons as he sprinted on the ragged edge of grass fringing the road, ready to follow the train as far as he could.

"I was only joking," Moses shouted after him.

Someone yelled at him, "Don't, don't!"

A hand caught the seam of his shirt, but he yanked it free and pushed on.

"You can't!"

"Where's his mother?"

He heard his mother shout back in triumph, "He knows it's just a superstition." The crowd gasped at her audacious claim and then a woman screamed as he grasped the rail and hoisted himself into the passenger car where the coffin bed had been placed.

For a moment, he held his breath, his heart thumping against his chest, and he looked out at the crowd. Ahead, the clouds slipped over the sun. Some of the people sniffed the air, and a few stepped back to claim the shelter of a tree.

"You are going to die!" He knew the voice before he saw his oldest brother, Solomon, come alongside as close as he could without touching the coffin train, his face twisted up with fear. Then Solomon turned to the crowd. "He is going to die," he repeated, swooping his arms around in a circle, as if he were winding them up. Others took up the chant, accusation and prediction and terror all wrapped up in one awful note, chugging like a train, "He is going to die, he is going die." But Joseph saw his mother, her long, proud neck rising high, smiling at him, and he was not afraid. He knew he was not going to die, he was free. Then, a sudden gust rattled through the scrub and before there was time to take another breath, the sky became a spout of gushing water.

People scattered to the trees and the servants dropped the ropes and went for the tarps tucked under the wagons. Joseph huddled in the padded box, smelling the tang of varnish and paint, and hoped no one would remember him. Then there was a whoosh as a tarp was thrown over the car, shutting out the light. But in the darkness he could still see the vision burning in his head, the driving wheels carved with petaled holes, the connecting rods and cranks and pistons that rose and fell as the train moved on, the coupling that joined one car to the next. He lay in the stuffy air, dreaming of a hundred cars winding through the village into the scrub.

The rain lightened, and he could hear voices under the wagon. "Have you thought how big a hole we'll have to dig to cover this beast?"

"How did it ever get so huge?"

"You didn't hear? Fatu Dendo told Mr. Sarbah if he was going to carve a train, he wanted to be sure it was just like the real ones Mr. Sarbah had ridden on in Europe and had Mr. Sarbah fly him there so he could see for himself."

Joseph startled. Not from Fatu Dendo's head, but someone else's, in a different country? He felt a bitterness in his stomach. His mother was right. He didn't belong in this village with its unfinished concrete huts and contented men resting in the shade. The voices kept on, but Joseph heard nothing else. He could only think of how he could get to the place where machines like this had been birthed. He wondered where Europe was. Perhaps it would be too far to walk and he would have to take a real train. The rain stopped thumping, and the tarp was pulled off, but Joseph lay there for a moment more, seeing himself jump on the very last car of a train picking up speed out of a station, and he began to travel far away from his brothers, farther than he could see, into an unknown world.

If he had thought about it then, he could have predicted what would happen a few minutes later when he climbed down from the train. The entire village shunned him, his brothers stopped talking to him, his teacher refused to have him in the class, the other children ran away when he walked down the lane, and he lived in happy silence for an entire year. But he would never have been able to imagine the miracle that happened when Mr. Sarbah finally learned of his stunt. Instead of being angry, the rich man was so proud of the folly his magnificent coffin had provoked, he pledged to pay for Joseph's entire education, first sending him to the mission school in Kumasi, then to high school in Accra. After he died, his son took over and arranged for Joseph to go to university and Joseph had flown on a plane to this cold, ancient city of arched bridges and train yards with tracks spreading out like fingers, and neatly squared curbs and old brick sidewalks and church steeples so high they were sometimes lost in the clouds, and now he was sitting in a smoky café across from a pale woman who had opened up another whole future in his head.

Monique had taken out the day's assignment and he watched her work on it, concentrating so hard her teeth bit into her colorless lips, and he wondered what they would taste like if he kissed her. The music was still drumming through the café, joined by the sound of laughter from a group of students in black leather jackets. One of them came over and asked Joseph for the empty chair at their table, and Joseph pushed it toward him, and then went back to staring at Monique.

Suddenly she closed her notebook and stuffed it into her bag hanging over the back of her chair. He watched helplessly as she went over and took her coat off the hook on the wall. "You have to go?" he asked when she came back for her bag. Something was wrong. She looked sour, mean even.

"I can't study here. I'm going to my place."

He hurried after her. "I'll walk you there."

She shrugged and tilted her head to a funny angle. "If you want."

Out in the street, the drizzle had started again. She took out an umbrella and popped it open, but he took it from her hands and held it over her as they walked, not caring that the rain soaked his face and jacket.

"You're getting wet." She hugged her bag in front of her and would not lift her eyes from the pavement.

"It's okay."

By the time they reached her apartment, he could feel his socks soggy in his squeaky shoes, and the front of his pants were thick and stuck to his thighs. He looked up at the building, trying to memorize the bland features, and finally saw two bright stripes from orange curtains hanging in one of the upper story windows. "Will you have coffee with me again?"

"I don't know." She looked down as she said it, pursing her lips together until they almost disappeared completely.

He thought he should have kissed her in the café right after she had taken a sip of hot coffee, but he remembered she did not put any sugar in hers and he winced for a moment, then decided it wouldn't matter.

"Can I have my umbrella?" The tiny pale blue marbles of her eyes were growing smaller now, closing down, contracting against the world, and he was desperate to find a way to bring her back but he didn't know how.

She unlocked the heavy glass door and swung it open, then it began to close sluggishly behind her with a loud pneumatic sigh. She had already started up the stairs when he caught the door and stuck his head inside the foyer. "Monique, Monique."

She stopped and leaned against the banister as if she were too tired to stand up, and when she looked down at him, he saw something strange flicker across her face. For a moment he did not speak while he looked at her and tried to understand what her face was saying. Was she dismissing him? Did she think he was not good enough for her? Then she tilted her head and with a finger she very slowly brushed the matted hair away from her face as if she didn't want him to notice. With that tentative gesture, it came to him. She thought he was teasing her. Oh no, she had it wrong, all wrong.

"I will tell you about the train, I promise. I will tell you everything," he pleaded. "Please, tomorrow—can we meet tomorrow? You'll see."

He felt his heart pounding in his chest and held his breath to shield himself from the blow of her refusal, but he saw relief relax over her face.

"Okay," she said, but she did not look at him and then he realized how shy she was, how gentle he would have to be.

Even though she had already turned around, he lifted his pink palm in a little wave. "Until tomorrow then." Behind him, the rain began to patter harder and louder on the cement, like a train gathering steam. He smiled and closed his eyes to listen for a moment, and then without waiting for the storm to weaken, he left the shelter of the doorway and started down the walk.

A. H. WALD has lived in North Africa since 2000. Her fiction has appeared in the *The Southern Review, North American Review, Image, Green Mountains Review, The William and Mary Review,* and *South Dakota Review,* as well as last year's collection of *The Best Christian Short Stories.*

To Jesus' Shoulder

by Andrew McNabb

In this seemingly whimsical story, we see not only a moment in the life of a narrator confronted with the sorrow of Christ's tortured death, but also the moment in his friend's life when contemplation of Christ and who He was becomes a jarring reality.

—Bret Lott

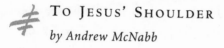

TO JESUS' SHOULDER
by Andrew McNabb

Charlie was always trying to do it some different way. Whenever he invited me for coffee, it was never to one of those trendy spots downtown but to a place that most would say had no character for drinking coffee, like the canteen in the parking lot on Marginal Way where the coffee came scalding hot in spongy Styrofoam cups, or the seventh floor of the library over at USM where the coffee poured from a vending machine just inside the double-door next to the elevator. And one time he even asked me to meet him at the 7-Eleven on Congress. We had an hour-long conversation just standing right there by the coffeepot, next to the Drake's cakes and the case of warm breakfast burritos.

And that was just coffee. There was the rest of Charlie to consider. Take the way he dressed, for example. I have no idea where he got his clothes. My guess is at Goodwill. Maybe that's not unusual, but what he wore was. It was always slightly frayed, and it was always colorful. He might wear red polyester slacks with a tartan shirt one time, and the next he might have an old gray suit coat over a lime green shirt so wrinkled you might think that was part of its design. Charlie would never say that he had a personal style, but I described him to himself one day as Delightfully Rumpled, and there was the nicest gleam in his eye over that.

And then there was the way he walked. He leaned back a tiny bit, as if he were going under the world's highest limbo setting. And his greetings. "How's the day?" he might say. Or, "How did it feel when you got up this morning?" Whatever he asked was always a surprise, and always, it seemed, intended to cause you to think about things in a different way.

But what was most unusual about Charlie was his questions. They could almost always be approached from two sides. At one of our recent meetings, Charlie wanted to discuss mail. He opened up the conversation by saying, "Is there anything more satisfying than that moment right before you drop a piece of mail into the mailbox? Check the address. Check the stamp. Open the lid, drop the mail, and *Clink*, you're done! *Voila!* Another task completed!" He stopped, paused, and looked into my eyes. "But then there's the rest of life until that next mailing." I don't know anyone else who ever thought of things that way.

Now, no one can do everything unconventionally. You still have to live somewhere, and you still have to eat, and unless you want to live in something like a yurt on a Mongolian steppe or in a closet in an old abandoned house, and subsist on a diet of bark or stones, you have to figure out how to fit into the system, at least a little bit. So Charlie worked part-time at a trinket store selling Maine paraphernalia to tourists—"I'm a scrimshaw man!" he'd say enthusiastically—and he always had interesting ways to think about what he did there, and to describe the type of people he met. "Do you know what it takes to talk the tourist talk?" he asked me one time. "Time!" was his answer, and he went into a long discourse about the different ways that could go.

It wasn't that I waited for his calls, but I did look forward to them, mostly because I don't do things the way Charlie does. And so when he called me last week and said, "To the Donut Cart!" I was excited to go. What would he tell me? How would he want me to deal with it?

It was a great spring day and I was happy to be out from work. I had been to the Donut Cart on many occasions, and had always seen it as just that, a steel cart with a man standing inside, serving donuts and coffee through a small window. Thinking that the cart may be today's topic, I attempted to analyze it, and how unusual it was for a man to be standing inside so small a tin cart, so small that he always looked unhappy and cramped. But the counter-balance to that was the beauty of the surroundings. And that, in turn, got me thinking further: Unlike all of the other places we had met—sandy parking lots, convenience stores, windowless cafeterias—this spot had a view. It was right up against Casco Bay, with nothing ugly in sight, just an unobstructed view of the water and the few small islands.

When I arrived at the Donut Cart, Charlie was already there.

He looked a little more rumpled than usual, but no less colorful. Orange corduroy pants and a buttonless vest over a white T-shirt. And then another new view for me: his arms from his biceps down were exposed. They were so thin and white.

As always, he started right in. "Sit, sit. Two parts today. One, did you ever think that maybe it's not all that bad to suffer? And two, did you know—and don't just automatically say yes or no—but did you know that there is a prayer to the shoulder wound of Jesus?" He flashed one of those little cards that people sometimes leave behind in phone booths or on tables at diners.

All I could think about was not the answer to the question, but how it was a different type of question. Quite different than, "Quick! What are the ingredients in a traditional Sevillian Bouillabaisse?" Or, "I'm glad you're here, now let's talk about how it feels to stand all day long."

Of course I had no idea there was such a prayer as one to the shoulder wound of Jesus, but before I even had time to answer, he said, "The shoulder wound! *Mon dieu!*"

And then, as he often would, Charlie went into an amalgam of thoughts and notions about the topic, telling me it might help if I thought of my own shoulder, its function, it being a joint attached to a socket and secured by tendons, muscle, and cartilage. "Hammer it down," he said, "with a great and heavy weight. Tear the flesh, boy!" He speculated that if there were a prayer to Jesus' shoulder wound, there must also be a prayer to the holes in His hands and in His feet and to the hole lanced in His side to ensure His death, but he didn't know for sure

and that didn't matter anyway because what was most interesting about this prayer, he said, was that it was the result of
an unrecorded suffering.

"What do you mean unrecorded?" I asked.

He flashed the card again. Someone named St. Bernard had
a personal conversation with Christ after Christ died, and St.
Bernard asked Christ what his greatest unrecorded suffering
was—and, of course, all I could think of was how St. Bernard
asked unusual questions, just like Charlie—and then Charlie
read a prayer that contained some of those very same words he
used, like flesh and bones laid bare and the crushing burden of
a cross. He huffed, and he sighed and he said, "Can you imagine
all that? Unusual. Unusual. A prayer to a *wound*."

Yes, it was an unusual day. And then we just sat there for the
longest time, silently, which was unusual in itself. In the past,
he would always have at least one addendum, like, "So, which
route will you take home tonight?" Or, "Now tell me again about
the day you were born." Instead, we just sat looking out at the
beautiful scenery, the sun high overhead and the cool wind floating in off the water, the caustic Donut Cart brew maybe serving
some type of purpose, tempering the surroundings, I guess, in
light of the shoulder wound and the suffering we were now supposed to consider.

Finally, after quite a deliberation, Charlie said, with a great
deal of levity, "To Jesus' shoulder!"

"To Jesus' shoulder," I replied. And, at least for that day right
there, that was that.

ANDREW MCNABB lives in an old house in the West End of
Portland, Maine, with his wife and four children. Whenever possible,
they walk to get where they're going. His stories have appeared in
The Missouri Review, New Delta Review, Many Mountains Moving,
and many other journals. He is currently at work on a book about
being a stay-at-home dad/writer/shaper of his children's future.

Midnight Clear

by Jerry B. Jenkins

The fact of all our lives is that other people are involved, and in this story we see that played out fully and mysteriously. Our decisions, however rational they may seem, affect other people, none more so than those we claim as family. "Midnight Clear" portrays two people who have reached their perceived ends with nothing to show for it save a loss of faith in themselves and, more importantly, God. But in their shared moment of crisis we see the blessing that understanding others can truly be.

—BRET LOTT

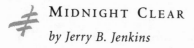

MIDNIGHT CLEAR
by Jerry B. Jenkins

He wrapped the Colt .44 magnum in an oily cloth he'd found in his glove box and stuffed it under the front seat. The station wagon, like Lefty, was running on empty.

He had traded four cans of gray, basement floor primer for the gun. Not a bad deal, he decided, since he had appropriated—as he liked to put it—the paint from his last employer. That was six weeks ago.

He hated guns. They were heavy, violent, uncontrollable things. Not unlike himself. A friend once let him shoot his .38 in the woods behind the trailer park. One shot had been enough. Loud and awful. The .44 was even bigger, more powerful. He'd heard that the victim would never hear the shot, especially if the victim himself had pulled the trigger.

That was his plan.

He was a loser. He knew it. His three ex-wives, his four kids (two by women he had never married), his dead father, and his aging mother knew it all too well. Everything he had ever touched had turned to dust. He was forty years old and had nothing to live for.

Merry Christmas.

The woman sat before the front window of her house. The room, like the house, was small; from where she sat she could see the back door off the kitchen. If she cared to look.

On her lap lay a guide to prescription drugs. She had the ingredients. She just didn't want them to taste bad or cause her any pain. What she wanted was a sleepy death that would look like an accident. Though she hoped her death would hurt the family that had hurt her so, she didn't want them to be embarrassed. The last thing she wanted was to be a burden.

That meant she would have to burn the guide. No one must know.

Evangeline was not one to beg. Sure, she wanted to see her children, especially on holidays. If they were too busy, that was all right. But how about a card, a call, something? How was it possible that her birthday had passed unnoticed? At Thanksgiving, not a word. And now Christmas.

But God bless that big church! She had received her only birthday mail from the Women's Missionary Society. Tonight the youth group had serenaded her with carols. They must have thought her tears were from joy, because she'd managed to smile as she wept.

There in her doorway she'd begged their forgiveness for not having hot chocolate or cookies, lying that her kids and grandkids had just left, and there were no leftovers. The sponsor, a tall young man with a goatee and a stocking cap, looked puzzled, blinking a time too many in the thin light from behind her.

"Sorry, but we thought you were a shut-in," he'd said. "We had it down that you haven't been to church for several weeks. But you look good."

"Been traveling," she said, lying again. "My kids are pretty spread out, you know."

But he didn't know. How could he? He and the kids were nice, but they hardly knew her name. And all their kindnesses made her family look only worse. Much as she tried to make excuses for her own kin, they had proved to her that she was worthless.

Lefty was merely cruising streets now, killing what little time he had left. He drove past a factory where he had once worked. He snorted. Some deal. Only place he ever got promoted. He'd celebrated by getting drunk, coming in late the next day, getting reprimanded and put on probation, then fired for arguing about it with his boss. Well, maybe a little more than arguing. That episode had cost him his second wife.

It also sent him back to AA. They always loved to see him; he was a classic. He could stay sober for months, but when he disappeared he might not turn up again for a year. Christmas Eve might be a fun night to surprise that bunch. There was always a crowd on holidays, and he would get the typical sympathetic welcome.

No. He didn't need that.

What he needed, he was sure, was a bullet to the brain. Sweet peace. Sweet relief. Unending sleep. He chuckled at the irony of the few singles in his pocket. To keep driving he would have to spend a few of them for gas. Every time he did that he lessened the quality of the booze he could afford to medicate himself in advance of the big moment. The alcohol would camouflage fear, he knew, and break down his natural resistance, dull his survival instinct. He talked himself out of taking a tall tale to AA before heading out for his pint and his private going-away party.

At a stoplight, he emptied his pockets and discovered he couldn't afford both gas and good booze. He drove to the only station he knew that didn't require paying first after dark, pumped himself four gallons, and drove off. Lefty wasn't even noticed. Story of his life.

Evangeline had never liked her name. She was the eldest of seven, born to a farmer who had ignored—to his everlasting regret—a call to the ministry. He had preached a little, done some local missionary work, and been an active layman most of his life. But he had disobeyed God, he told his children—Evangeline, Matthew, Mark, Luke, Chastity, Ruth, and Cletus—and that's why his crops were seldom blessed.

Poor Clete, Evangeline thought. The only kid born late enough to escape Daddy's trying to make up to God by naming his kids like saints, and he winds up with a moniker like that.

Evangeline had been devout in her teens. Something clicked for her at the little country church, and she had shed tears of true repentance and dedication. God became personal. Jesus was a Friend she could talk to and live for. But how long ago had that been? And what had happened?

Her daddy had been caught with the wife of his hired man, and though he'd denied everything till the day he died, Evangeline had known the truth. She could see it in her mama's eyes. Maybe that's what made Evangeline run off with the first man who said he loved her.

It had been a mistake from the beginning, but divorce was not an option in those days. Not like now. She liked to say she had stopped counting the divorces her six kids had between them. But she hadn't stopped: fourteen, and only one son still with his first wife.

Evangeline had raised the kids with no money and with a man who ignored her and with whom she fell out of love. She hadn't complained. She had made her choice, and she had a job to do.

Unfortunately, that job consisted of thousands of unending tasks. She did everything for everybody in the house, from making scant rations feed the crowd to sewing and washing everyone's clothes to cleaning up after every last one of them.

Why had she done it? Other women in her situation let their places go. She couldn't do that. Though her kids took her for granted and even criticized her, the work gave her life structure, a framework, a reason. She kept at the work of keeping house until the children left, and her husband died.

She had been able to get the kids to go to church with her only until they were about twelve. Then each followed the others' example and dropped out. Now, when weather permitted, Evangeline went to church alone. But it was a six-block walk to the bus. She'd gone to the Women's Missionary Society once and gotten on their roll. That resulted in the occasional card or we-missed-you note.

How she longed for a message like that from even one of her kids. But they were busy, had their own lives.

Snow started, and accumulated quickly. Lefty heard the crunching under his tires whenever he drifted to the shoulder. He wanted to see the town from his favorite perch at lovers' lane on his last night on earth. He pulled into a spot in a long line of cars with fogged windows. The lights below made him think of

Bethlehem. He heard the famous song every year, but when was the last time he had thought about Bethlehem?

There had been a stretch when he took his two older boys to Sunday school and church. He even went himself a few times. When he was a kid, he prayed with a teacher and she told him he'd been saved. He didn't understand it then and didn't want to think about it now. Far as he could remember, he'd never had a prayer answered. Not one. Either the whole deal was a sham, or he had missed some crucial detail.

His resolve only grew as he sat there watching the snow build on the hood of his Dodge. Every time he restarted the drafty old rig to clear the window and get a little heat on the floor, the engine knocked and rattled.

Someone tapped on the window, and shined a flashlight through Lefty's window.

"You alone, pal?" the man said, and Lefty saw the shiny brim of the cop's hat, the badge on the front of his jacket.

Lefty nodded and smiled sheepishly.

"You some kind of pervert?" the cop said.

Lefty's smile vanished. "I'll move along if you want."

"That's what I want."

A nobody trying to be a somebody, Lefty thought. He said things like that aloud only when he was lubricated. Then he could claim it had been the booze talking. And he would be right. He never had to own up to anything.

He didn't want to go to a bar, and he was sure the package

liquor stores would close by midnight. Lefty decided to buy his pint before making one last pass of his childhood home. What a dump that was! Few fond memories there.

Evangeline was surprised to find herself hungry on this last night. Who would have thought the body would still crave nourishment when the end was near? She slowly walked to the kitchen and pulled hard on the handle of the old refrigerator. The thing should have died years ago.

Inside she found a lone pickle spear in a jar of juice. She couldn't remember when she'd bought that jar. Next to it sat a half-empty can of cat food, waiting for a kitty that had not come back from a date with Tom two weeks before. A leftover piece of chicken that had to be at least three weeks old lay on a plate.

She closed the fridge, then put a small pan of water on the stove. She rummaged for an ancient jar of bouillon cubes she knew had to be stale, despite their individual wrappings. When the water was near boiling she crumbled a cube into a cup. Indeed, stale. But all she wanted was the salty beef taste. Fresh or not, it would taste the same. How like her own history.

And how ironic this last supper. When she allowed herself to dream of her childhood, her happy memories revolved around the great dining room table. No one ate like farm men, and on

Sundays, no one ate like a farmer's family. Chicken and ham both, lots of potatoes, steaming bowls of beans and carrots and squash, pies and cakes and cookies too.

Evangeline had tucked away a particularly precious mental picture of her mother smiling adoringly at her father, pretrouble, as he told a guest missionary that he had not lost sight of his call and that he might yet one day follow God to the ends of the earth.

That day they were one big, happy, well-fed family. Just as the family she herself had raised had never been. Well-fed, maybe, but never harmonious. Alcohol had done that. No interest in church had done that. No father image had done that. But then she had grown up with a positive father model—at least for a time—and look how she turned out.

"Merry Christmas," the clerk said, bagging Lefty's pint. "Hope you've got somebody to share this with tonight."

"You want a pull?" Lefty said, and began to take it from the sack.

"No, no," the man said. "Just makin' conversation. Hate to see a man drink alone, 'specially on Christmas Eve."

If you only knew what else I was doing tonight!

He'd once prided himself on finishing his bottle before passing out. No risk of spillage or theft. No waste. Tonight it was himself he would waste. If there was a swallow or two left in the bottle, who would care? If he knew the answer to that, he wouldn't have had a .44 under the seat.

"What am I waiting for?" Evangeline said out loud as she sat by the window again. There was enough sodium Pentothal and Phenobarbital in her various prescriptions to kill a twelve-hundred-pound thoroughbred inside thirty seconds. The crystalline powder was odorless, so it would probably be tasteless. She would mix it with the bouillon, and then she would be gone. Painlessly.

It would be frightening but quick, and she could do it. Evangeline had decided that having no reason to live was reason enough to die. Before adding the poison, she sipped delicately at the hot bouillon, and the memories flooded back. Was it too much to expect that Jesus would accept her on Christmas Eve, even if she chose this most heinous way of getting to heaven? *Would* she get there? She didn't know. It would be nice, but the point of this trip was not where she was going; it was what she was leaving.

Despite the destruction alcohol had brought him, Lefty couldn't deny the thrill of unsacking a fresh bottle, breaking the seal by unscrewing the cap, smelling the essence—once in a great while—of the really good stuff, the kind that started, not ended, a binge. This was the stuff that would be both friend and lover and promise you anything.

Having been on the wagon since the day he had last worked, his throat was primed. In a little while he would savor the moment, play it out, open this bottle like a gift. Good stuff deserved ceremony, for it was a facilitator of the trip to oblivion.

Lefty packed the sack under his seat and heard it clink against the weapon. Now *there* was a combination of goodies. One quick and the other deadly. He would drive past his childhood home, return to lovers' lane, suck down the pint before the cop came back, and do the deed. *That,* officer, if you must know, is how I get my kicks.

The bouillon was gone. Evangeline was weary. She set her cup on the small table before the window, folded her hands in her lap, lowered her head, and let her shoulders slump. Her lie to the singers nagged at her. Did she need to confess it to have any chance of heaven? She didn't know. She simply wanted to get it over with and find out.

The old woman took her cup to the kitchen, turned the heat on under the water again, and rinsed out her cup. She unwrapped another square of bouillon and set it next to the cup. While the water heated, she moved to the bathroom where she studied her prescriptions. She transferred half a dozen capsules from each of two bottles and put them into a third. She didn't know how heat would affect them. She would not mix them in until her new drink began to cool.

She went back to the kitchen and heard one of the very few cars that went by that night. No Christmas parties in this neighborhood.

No Christmas tree at his mother's home, Lefty noticed. Well, he hoped she hadn't expected him to provide one. He didn't have one either. He guessed his mother liked Christmas, though. Too bad. Looked like she was in bed. There was a light on in the tiny living room, but no one in there. The light from the kitchen looked dim, the one over the stove she always left on. The rest of the place was dark.

Where did the other people on this street get money for decorations? They were as poor as his mother. Probably credit cards. Same things that nearly ruined him. He should have used one for the spree he'd planned for this night, he thought. By the time they caught him, he'd be farther gone than they could imagine.

He was excited about his plan, but bone weary nonetheless. Something about doing nothing and having nowhere to go had left him logy and listless for longer than he could remember. It would be so good to be rid of that feeling.

He drove around the block, wanting one last look at the old place with its leaning, one-car garage and tiny backyard with the broken swingset. When he came around again, he pulled onto the shoulder across the street and stared. What would be wrong with cracking open the pint for a preliminary sniff? He reached beneath the seat, hoping no one would see him and call the cops.

Evangeline waited until the water and the bouillon were tepid before stirring in the lethal dose. An autopsy would show what she had ingested, but without a note or any sign of distress, her demise would be ruled an accident. She could do at least that much for her children.

She carried her lukewarm cup to the living room, set it daintily on a mismatched saucer, and sat again. She had turned up the thermostat earlier and now buttoned her sweater, but she wondered if that would make her body decompose too quickly. She didn't want that. She wanted to appear to be sleeping in her chair by the window, and when no one could rouse her with the phone or doorbell, they would just break in and take her away. No trouble. Not much bother. Nothing distasteful.

A car idled on the shoulder across the street one that hadn't been there when she had gone to the kitchen. Looked like Luschel's old crate.

Her boy, Luschel. Lefty, as he insisted on being called.

With the cap off, the aroma of the whiskey hit him. It was all he could do to keep from inhaling the liquid as well. Strange, the stuff that had nearly killed him before he could do it himself smelled almost worth living for. But he wouldn't drink it yet. He would save it for a farewell hit before the farewell shot.

He replaced the cap and the bottle and the sack and glanced up with a start to see his mother in her chair by the window. She couldn't see him, he knew, so he looked hard and long at her as he hadn't done for years.

What had so effectively removed her from the forefront of his mind? When he'd left home twenty years before, he'd seemed to think of her every day. Even called her frequently. But how long had it been? Would she feel betrayed if he left this life without even a good-bye?

He owed her at least that.

When the car door opened, the figure getting out sure looked like Luschel. Older, heavier, slower than she remembered, but as he carefully made his way across the street, she knew it was him. Had he had some premonition about her? Would he be able to tell somehow that her death was in the cup of bouillon on the table? This would have been easier if she had not had to face a living, breathing reminder of why she was doing it.

But he had come. He had apparently made a decision to see her, and driven here. His visit wouldn't change her mind, but it was something. She fought the urge to ask a litany of questions she knew were only complaints: Where have you been? Why haven't you called? Why do I hear all my news about you from others? Don't you love me anymore? Did you forget my birthday? Why no call at Thanksgiving?

For some sad but delicious reason, she waited until she heard his knock before rising. The outside lights were off, so she could pretend not to have seen him approach. She even peered out through the crack with the door chain locked, as if to determine who it was.

"It's me, Mom."

"Luschel!"

"Lefty, Mom."

"Let's not fight," she said too quickly, she knew, then led him to a chair next to the one she'd been sitting in what suddenly seemed all night long. "Throw your coat anywhere."

"I'll leave it on," he said, and shrugged. "Just came to say Merry Christmas."

Suddenly Evangeline could not speak. He had come to wish her a good holiday? Was this sentiment she felt, or anger? The latter, surely, because the list of accusations against him was on the tip of her tongue. She imagined herself screaming, *I'm killing myself tonight, tonight, because of you!* and his whining, *Me, Ma? What'd I do?* And she'd tell him it was what he hadn't done, and he'd say, *What about the others?*

Well, the others were just as guilty. But he was the one who was here. He was the embodiment of the ills of the family. For some reason it had all fallen apart. They had drifted, become no-accounts, made messes of their lives. Evangeline knew she was as much to blame as anyone, but she had tried. How could they treat her this way when she had tried so hard?

They sat, and he saw how old his mother looked. In fact, she didn't look well. She seemed distracted, upset. What could he say that she would remember after he was gone? It would have to be something that wouldn't hurt her and yet wouldn't seem later to have been a lie.

"Actually, what I really came over for was to get a Merry Christmas from you."

She stared. "You want me to wish you a—"

"No, I mean—" he paused, and shrugged again. "I just figured if I could come and see my ma it would be a Merry Christmas for me." He crossed his arms, looked at his feet. "Kind of selfish, I guess."

What a wonderful thing to hear! What a strange thing for him to say! It was not like him to be emotional or even expressive.

"I don't think you're selfish," she said, and now she too crossed her arms and looked at the floor. She'd wanted to add, *You sure have been over the years, and what am I supposed to think when I never hear from you?* But if being with her was what he wanted for Christmas, that was easy.

She looked up at him. She couldn't resist pushing it a little, the compliment had felt so good. "Why do I make it a Merry Christmas?"

He looked up then too, and Evangeline could see in his eyes that she had pushed too far. He looked past her, self-conscious, she knew. "I don't know," he said. "Because you're my ma. That's all."

"Well," she said, "I have to admit, you're the best thing that's happened to me all night."

"Why?"

She shrugged. She didn't want to get into it. Was there something on his mind? Some real reason for his visit? Did he need cash? She wouldn't have given him a dime if she had a hundred bucks. Which she didn't.

Evangeline remembered the night he had come screaming from inside her, a precious child born into turmoil. Had he ever had a happy season, a time when family problems didn't cloud his eyes? She didn't even know what to ask him anymore to simply make conversation. Like her, his spouses and his children were painful subjects.

"I'm glad you came," she tried. "I needed to see one of my children this Christmas."

So there it was, she had said it. She had indicted them all, even him. But had he caught it? She couldn't tell. She found a loose strand of yarn at the elbow of her sweater and twisted it. She wanted to touch him, to embrace him, to comfort him if he needed her. But she also wanted him to go so she could be about her business, the business of finality.

She needs me? It was the last thing Lefty'd expected. Now *that* was a complicator. Needed was something he hadn't felt for he couldn't remember how long. What did she need him for? So she could see one of her children? *One of her children. I'm one of her children.* It was a curious word for a middle-aged drunk about to do away with himself. I am a child. Her child. Someone will miss me.

"What are you drinking?" he asked, to break the tension, and nodded at the cup on the table.

"Bouillon. But it's cold." It seemed she tried to smile.

"I don't mind," he said, reaching for it. "Long as it's wet."

But his mother snatched it from his hand, making it spill.

"I've already drunk from it," she lied, "and I have a cold."

Evangeline stood and took the cup to the kitchen, her hands shaking. Wouldn't that have been a sorry way to go, poisoned by your own mother's suicide potion? She sniffed it. He would never have been able to tell. But what would he think when he heard what had killed her?

What had made her so jumpy? When she asked from the kitchen if he wanted her to make him a fresh cup, he said, "No, I got to get going," and cleared his throat. This was becoming awkward. They hadn't interacted as mother and son since he was in elementary school. Too much had been said and done over the years. Nothing would ever be the same. His plan was best. He needed to get on with it.

He was going? She had just gotten used to the idea that he might stay awhile. But no, this was all right. She still had her cup. She had betrayed nothing. It would still look like an accident. Twenty minutes before she wouldn't have guessed he'd have cared. "Well, okay, good-bye then," she said, returning.

Lefty had expected her to protest. He cocked his head, realizing she'd accepted his farewell, and stood. He zipped his coat and turned to the door.

"Thanks for coming," his mother said. "It meant a lot to me."

He put his hand to the doorknob, then turned and said, "Well, I'm glad, but as I say, I came for me."

I came for me. The words suddenly meant more to Evangeline than she could say. He looked so forlorn, so sad, standing there. Because of her decision to take her own life, she was unsure where she would stand with God. That bothered her a whole lot less than wondering about Luschel and his future.

"You going to church anywhere?" she asked, and thought for some reason of the youth group and the young pastor who'd thought she was a shut-in.

"Church?" he said. He shook his head. "Not for a long time."

She wanted to urge him to go, but that had never worked. She wanted to recommend her church, because though it was big and a little impersonal, he might like it. But she couldn't mother him, not now. It was way too late. Maybe if he thought he was doing it for her? No, he'd see through that. But what if she could just tell him about it somehow? If she mentioned it, and then he found out she was dead, maybe he would remember and go, out of sentiment.

"I like my church," she said. "But I can't walk six blocks to the bus when it's so cold and icy. Could you give me a ride sometime? I haven't been in a while." She hated pretending she would even be alive Sunday, but if it got him into church . . .

She felt like such a hypocrite. The world would be better off without her, she decided. Lying to get her son back to church!

His mom, the only real Christian in the family, couldn't even get out to church? After the way they'd treated her all these years, nobody was around to give her a ride? Lefty knew what he had to do. He would leave a note that she should be given his car. It wasn't much, but it would be something.

Then it hit him. That car would be a mess that could never be cleaned up. He would have to do this outside the car, standing in the cold in the middle of nowhere. That was no way to die. But what kind of thinking was that? Who cared? He was going crazy, a fading loser in the middle of the night, trying to get out of his mother's house so he could kill himself, and worrying over leaving her a clean car like it was some sort of Christmas gift.

Why not leave life and his mother with a ray of hope, something for her to go on? Sure, she'd resent him for it in the morning when the awful news came, but it would temporarily give her a Merry Christmas.

"Tell you what, Ma," he said, and let go of the doorknob. "You need a ride to church, you call me. I'll take you. I'm not promising I'll go in or nothing. But I'll get you there."

He saw her eyes begin to fill, then heard a catch in her throat. "You'd do that for me?" she said.

He looked away. "I said I would, didn't I?"

He needs me! she decided.

Lefty moved carefully back across the street and noticed the snow had stopped. The sky was clear, the stars illuminating the blanketed ground. He turned to wave at his mother.

He drove to an abandoned bridge and dropped the gun into the icy water. And then he surprised himself. Without even removing it from the sack, Lefty tossed the pint in too.

He was still a no-account loser, and he wasn't sure he would ever be anything else. But his mother needed him. And for once in his life, he would be there.

JERRY B. JENKINS is the author of more than 170 books. His writing has appeared in *Time, Reader's Digest, Parade, Writer's Digest,* and dozens of Christian periodicals. He owns the Christian Writers Guild and Jenkins Entertainment, a filmmaking company that has produced this story as a feature film starring Stephen Baldwin. Jerry and his wife live in Colorado and have three grown sons and four grandchildren.

Going to Jackson

by Janice Daugharty

*In this dark and haunting story, we see how evil
and its aftermath can test the faith of believers and
nonbelievers alike. Velda Crandell's apathy toward
God is understandable, given the ongoing test of
her belief in Him that continues for as many years
as it does. Yet the mercy she has experienced from
God is reflected in her sympathy, finally, for her
husband's murderer.*

—Bret Lott

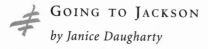

GOING TO JACKSON

by Janice Daugharty

She's been told that it might actually happen this time. She's been told that before.

Velda Crandell's last living son is driving her hood-heavy Olds, taking her to Jackson, fifty miles south of Atlanta, and it seems a waste of time and gas. It's a fine day, a working day, Tuesday, May 6, 2003, and Willis has taken off from his job at BellSouth where he works repairing phone lines on the outskirts of Albany, home of all the Crandells, what's left of them.

On a hill across a choppy green pasture, east of the Interstate, magnolias on uniform trees each side of a little white church are beginning to puff out their creamy petals, boasting blood-red hearts. The trees top-out even with the steeple, perfect balance, perfect picture. A place where good people gather on Sunday. Used to, Velda bought into that, but now she knows that people are not good and fire ants fester in the hidden dips of the pasture and magnolias fall to the ground and turn brown after only a couple of days. She has tried not to show her family that bitter side of herself, her brooding they mistake for calm. The only way to make sense of life is to expect nothing, she figures, keep it simple, wring each day of its pleasures, even if it's just food and drink. Proof looms up before her as a billboard sign replaces the church picture with the message "Magnolia Plantation, fresh orange juice, 2 miles, exit 89."

To counter that dread feeling of somebody stepping on her grave before Donald Jacobs can be executed, she speaks to Willis. "Seems like a waste, don't it?"

"What's that, Mama?" Willis is a big man—he has high blood. How come his face is red and bloated? Him not even fifty yet and he looks like he's sixty.

"Us going to Jackson again." In the side mirror, Velda can see her Linda's faded red car. Sun glaring on the windshield prevents Velda from seeing her daughter's face. Following Linda's car are the other automobiles belonging to various members of the Crandell clan, about a dozen heading north up I-75 for Jackson. Again.

"This time he's gonna fry," says Willis. He flips the sun visor from above the windshield to his window where the sun is beginning to shine in his eyes. In the west, fields of red cattle graze seeding brown winter rye.

At home they'd left pale clouds with wind herding them across an underlit sky. Now feathery gray clouds sweep across the sky. Framed in the windshield, they touch tips and overlap, creating dark thunderheads.

Killer storms in the Midwest and parts of the South, war just over in Iraq. Now all the TV news can do is jaw over what was, show what was. The burned body of a young Iraqi boy has been shown so many times that Velda sometimes feels as if she is the one wrapped in gauze with only her eyes showing like water reflecting somebody else's eyes, somebody on hold, waiting for fate to make up its mind to go ahead and be done with her or to give her another chance.

"That was last time he was supposed to get the chair. They're talking lethal injection this go-round." Velda needs to set the record straight for her own ordering of mind—thirty-one years is a long time to be doing the same thing, any thing, over and again. She's lost track of the number of appeals, the lawyers' tricks that led up to the appeals, how many times Donald Jacobs has been sentenced to death, then walked. The latest appeal by Jacobs's lawyer is one she will never forget because of its rock-bottom reaching, their desperation, which gives her the most hope. A minister's prayer at the opening of Jacob's 1988 retrial in Houston County Superior Court was not recorded, Jacob's lawyer says, so he argues that it was impossible for the defense to challenge it. In the prayer, the minister's divine plea that God's will be done had prejudiced the jury against Jacobs. A stay of execution should be granted.

"Thy will be done," she intones. How all prayers and blessings over food end at the Crandell family reunions each spring. It means nothing; it's a figure of speech that has lost its power to move.

Willis's stout legs in creased khakis are laid out, and his left foot in a brown loafer and worn tan sock leans to one side.

What is he thinking? Maybe about that hot autumn day after his daddy and brothers died and some politician looking for votes had fitted a flatbed truck with the State's only electric chair. Exhibited it at schools all over Georgia, using the excuse that he intended to scare young people out of choosing a life of crime.

Just seeing the chair, Willis had primed his mind to expect next-day executions of the Jacobses and their gang. Then next month, then next year, then soon. He had been a boy possessed. Kept scrapbooks. Is a true-crime reader to this day.

Maybe now Willis would as soon Donald Jacobs be led into the execution chamber, strapped down, then at the last minute, be unstrapped and led back to his holding cell on death row? He has his own problems, Willis does. His wife, Brenda Gail, has left him and moved to Miami, Florida, taking with her their boy and girl. Said she was sick of living in the "public eye." Well, they all are. Good luck to him if Willis can make it from south Georgia to south Florida, twelve hours on the road, on a weekend, to visit his children and still hold down his job so he can sweat out monthly child-support payments.

Justice has taken too long to be served. So long that Velda and her entire family have almost grown out of the mood for revenge.

Not only does Velda have trouble recalling the face of Donald Jacobs, she has trouble recalling the faces of her husband, Ned, his brother Albert, her two sons and her daughter-in-law, all slaugh-tered like hogs on butcher day over a quarter of a century ago.

The pillared red brick Magnolia Plantation shows to the right of the interstate. *Free* fresh orange juice.

Suddenly it comes to Velda—she sits up straight—that she's not afraid Jacobs won't die this time, she's afraid that he will. Then, what dwelling point of equal challenge will keep her and her family going till the end of their lives?

Velda had been working in the school lunchroom the day it hap-pened and she can still see the huge stew pot she was scouring in the tub-size sink when she heard. She can see her face reflected on the pot, its silly egg-stood-on-end shape, like looking in a fun-house mirror. The broadened bridge of her nose, and the nose itself spread, exaggerated as if to mock her worst features. Things all turned around. She can smell the sour lemony dish detergent in the government gallon jug that she'd had such trouble lifting with her wrenched right arm. Maybe she'd broken a bone when she had stuck her hand through the wire fence to pet one of the cows and it had flung its red head and rammed her forearm into a wood post. No money and no time for doc-tors—the arm would have to heal on its own. It seemed that everything in the lunchroom was oversized and required lifting, straining with. Over the years, that fun-house face, that lemony smell, and the strain of lifting have lingered with her imaginings of how it happened, a good deal of which she knows from facts of the case. The rest she's filled in, filled in and worn out the images, the words, the actions. She's not sure anymore of what is fact and what is of her own conjuring.

May 14, 1973: the two Jacobses, Donald and Ronald, and their buddies Inman Hiers and Wilson Tole had escaped from a Maryland prison. The car they had stolen ran out of gas just a ways up the dirt road from the house where Velda and her husband, Ned, and their two youngest children lived. The other sons and their wives lived in trailers on the home place, working the farm with Ned and Velda.

Willis and Linda were still in school. He was fourteen then and she was just eight, her daddy's pet baby, as he called her.

The faceless four in the stalled car that morning had gotten out, stumping around, smoking stolen cigarettes, swigging whiskey, and peeing like dogs on the car tires. The sheriff had told that last bit of information on the witness stand as if it explained something vital about their characters, and for Velda it had.

She used to put filthy words in their mouths, imagining what had been said. But over the years, the words, like their faces, had gotten too jarring on her sanity.

Donald Jacobs, the ringleader, the meanest, the boldest, suddenly recalled passing an old house down the road. Maybe some gas in one of the tractors under the shelter he remembered seeing south of the house.

"Don't look like people'd own nothing," said his brother, "but can't never tell."

"Ain't nothing more despiteful than a dad-bummed bunch of church-going farmers," Donald had said, according to Ronald, who later turned State's evidence to save his own hide (he served twelve years and was released to start over again because he'd had a bad life, meaning a tough upbringing).

If only they'd gone to the shelter and siphoned the gas from the tractor and left . . . But that was just one more of Velda's what-ifs in the middle of the night. It did no good, it changed nothing.

At the lane leading up to the old unpainted farmhouse, set back off the dirt road, one of them had opened the mailbox and left it open. That's what the mail carrier told. (Velda never left her mailbox open.) And told that she must have come by, dropping off their light bill and a few sale circulars, a Penney's catalogue with a woman in a short green linen skimmer on the front. That very time the escaped cons had been inside, slinging pots and pans and dumping dresser drawers and overturning chairs and mattresses. Looking for money. They ate some of the biscuits Velda had baked that morning, the sidemeat she had fried. Both dishes Velda had left covered on the kitchen table for Ned and the boys and Mary to eat when they came in from hoeing the tobacco in the back field. Mary, always dieting, would have to eat biscuits or starve. It seemed that Velda was always cooking, if not for her own family, then for the five hundred or so students at the school in Sylvester, ten miles away.

Lined up and walking, Donald Jacobs and his gang's shoe prints were dug into the soft sandy dirt of the lane when Ned and the boys and Mary came in for lunch. It was dry—Velda could remember that—and the Crandells were worried that their disturbing the dirt with their hoes would cause the hot sun to draw what little moisture was left from the last rain and sips of nighttime dew. But if they didn't hoe, the weeds and grass would take over the tobacco. It was a gamble, Ned said, anyway you looked at it. Next tobacco crop, he and his brother Albert would buy an irrigation outfit on time. Cutting down on the odds against bringing tobacco to its maturity. Such a long way from seedlings, to ripe tobacco, to the warehouse and sale in July and August.

Mary was in front of the pickup with her father-in-law, Ned, and her husband, the youngest Crandell boy on back with his brother and uncle, when Ned drove through the opening of the balking wire gate from the fields behind the house. Over the whine and ping of the old primer-gray truck's engine, they could hear the sliding, bumping, hauling and smashing inside the house.

"Wonder what all *that's* about," Ned said to Mary, pulling up to the side porch and parking the pickup under the dinosaur live oak that shaded the north side of the house. Next to the porch steps, Velda's white hen and biddies were jigging and pecking at potato peels and onion skins from last night's beef stew, not even noticing the rumbling in the house, so used to noise were they with a family the size of Velda's banging in and out of doors.

Ned bumped open the sprung truck door with the hardened heel of his hand and got out, leaving it open.

The boys on back bailed off, resetting their caps and staring at the house and the knocking rumble of the men about their mischief inside. No car or truck in the sunny front lane. No sign of anybody.

"Hey!" Ned yelled. "What's up in there?" He was a giant of a man in loose denim bib overalls, which he claimed were cooler for working. He liked them loose for the air to circulate and keep the insides of his thighs from chapping. He had sugar in his blood and was plagued with yeast between his thighs, especially during summer. It got so bad at times that Velda had to bundle his bull-sized testicles in gauze, a job she loved because it always led to more. Big and tough-talking as he was, Ned could be tender with her. Sometimes he tried to make her jealous— women were always after the Crandell men. But Velda was never jealous, she was proud of the good-looking man she had married, proud of the sons she had given him. Besides, she said often to Ned, who but me would be fool enough to take on this job of farmwife, nursemaid, and cook?

The boys, and Mary now, just stood wondering, listening.

Suddenly the racket inside stopped. Like a TV muted. Katydids' pealing in the high grass along the lane reached ear-cringing pitch. The hen softly clucking and her biddies peeping were calming familiar sounds, like the potash smell of the marled gray dirt of the yard, the clean smell of moss draping the trunk-sized branches of the live oak.

"Maybe Willis come home from school." Albert had a white rag tucked under his cap because when he worked he rained sweat. "Willis, that you?" he hooted.

Trying to make light of the situation, Mary's husband, Benny, laughed. "Wouldn't be Willis, not and us hoeing tobacco today. Scared he might have to help."

Nobody else laughed. They didn't even look at him, and Benny's eyes remained fixed on the narrow, unpainted side porch and the open kitchen door. The porch floor was tracked with sand, and he knew his mother always swept the front and side porches before heading out to work.

"Probably some kids. Skipped school to mess around," Mary said. The men were creeping toward the doorsteps leading up to the porch, and she followed.

"You best come on out," Ned shouted. He hoped it was school younguns. He knew it wasn't.

They all stopped, listening. Nothing. No sound inside the house. All was so quiet they could hear from the living room mantel the weary Seth Thomas ratchet into its rollover purring rhythm.

The oldest boy, Robbie, headed back to the truck and took a crowbar from the bed, then returned to where the others were standing. "Mary," he said, lifting the bar in a tight grip, "you get on back in the truck, hear?"

Mary turned and walked to the truck, leaning on the front bumper with her arms crossed. Her hips in dirty worn-out blue jeans looked wider spread against the bumper. She could see the Crandell men on the porch now, walking toward the open door of the dim kitchen. The rattle of the locusts in the oak grew shriller, deafening in the stillness. The chickens under the porch now began cackling, and the biddies gathered around the hen.

"Who's there?" Ned in the doorway shouted.

A loud explosion blew him back into the boys and Albert following and they all scattered, leaping off the edges of the porch in all directions. Their faces set in expressions of fear and surprise. Too soon for sorrow over their slumped father and brother in the doorway. Another explosion, an orange flashette, and Albert went down at the west corner of the porch. More shots and now Mary could see the slender, young, brown-haired man with what looked like Ned's deer rifle standing in the doorway. Benny dropped facedown on the humped roots of the live oak, left side of the truck; Robbie lunged for Mary, shocked stiff on the truck bumper. His right hand raked her left leg as he fell like somebody tripped, facedown, too, eyes open and staring at his brother crumpled but crawling around the roots of the old oak. The next shot got him in the spine, ricocheting to the scabby trunk of the oak and chunks of bark rained down on Benny's body.

Mary suddenly roused from her stupor and ran around to the rear of the pickup, screaming for help. Just help, "Help!"

"Go get her," Donald Jacobs on the porch shouted inside. He was holding the shotgun out before him.

Mary started running, crying, toward the mailbox and the

road. Running with all her strength and seeing the dirt streaming under her feet. The strange line of shoe tracks she couldn't take her eyes off of.

Halfway up the lane, two of the men tackled her from behind. The Jacobses' buddies, Inman and Wilson. They smelled of whiskey and unwashed bodies, like the septic tank seepage at her and Benny's trailer she was forever complaining about but likely never would again.

Somebody was laughing; she was crying.

"Bring her on back," Donald called from the porch. "Have us a little fun, what y'all say?" (Velda used to spice up what they said during those ventures into her imagination, but she'd never been exposed to such and figured she had it all wrong, that it was worse and she couldn't go there because she'd never been and then she wished she'd made something special for Mary's lunch. Steamed okra and tomatoes wouldn't have taken much time.)

Screaming, biting, kicking, Mary was dragged toward the house, up the porch steps, and over her father-in-law's massive side-slung body. Without breath he looked shrunk. She never thought he liked her, she thought he could read her mind. She'd kept her distance till now . . . now stepping right over him. His work-scarred hands were outstretched as if to shield off the bullets.

Mary was an orphan, a charity child, raised in a Christian boarding school. No family, and when she married Benny it was as if she'd married his whole bossy family. Sick of them all, one Sunday at dinner, their quarreling disguised as teasing, she had set out crying up the lane, heading for she didn't know where.

It was Mr. Ned who came after her in the truck. He just pulled up alongside and leaned across the seat and opened the door for her to get in. She did because there was nothing else to do—besides, she really loved Benny.

Mr. Ned patted her left shoulder, speaking low, as if to prevent spooking her. "Cry, little gal, cry if you want to. But I'm taking you home where you belong."

Court records: Donald Jacobs and his gang took turns raping Mary Crandell on the carefully made-up bed in the main bedroom of the house.

Maybe Mary thought at that point that they would just rape her and let her go, or take her with them as a hostage. But they dragged her out to the Crandell truck and drove her to the tobacco field and there they raped her again, then shot her like target practicing at a motion-rigged scarecrow as she ran down the long heat-shimmering rows of the clean-hoed and withering tobacco watered only with Crandell sweat.

Linda's red car eases up in the left lane of I-75, then pulls in front of Willis and Velda in the outside lane. Immediately she switches on her right blinker to signal that she is about to exit.

"Bathroom stop," says Willis, chuckling. "Women!"

Velda laughs but doesn't like what he's said. "Them growing boys of hers after something to tide them over till they can get to Denny's for supper."

Linda swerves onto the exit ramp and motors up the crescent drive to the front of the rest stop. Opens the door and gets out, heading for the breezeway of the new red brick building with ladies' and men's restrooms on each side. She has on white pants and a blue shirt and cheap but stylish brown sandals slapping at her heels.

Willis parks to the right of her car, and the other cars and pickups behind begin filling the empty parking slots. Sitting with their engines idling. All along the curved concrete curbing and mowed grass, Velda can see inside the cars and trucks the heads of her grandchildren, nieces and nephews. Some bobbing, some leaning, some bowed as if praying. Future Crandell men and women.

Most children she knew feared television-bred spooks, teachers, their parents and the law. The Crandell children feared the Jacobses. Donald Jacobs was their Santa Claus and Halloween spook wrapped up in one. He could bring joy and he could bring terror. If he got executed this go-round, May 6, 2003, at 6 PM, their whole family would celebrate at Denny's, and the Crandells, what was left of them, could have peace, though Velda couldn't imagine it. She couldn't imagine what her family would be happy and sad about after Donald Jacobs died.

Three of the women get out of their cars and walk toward

the rest stop, grouping in the way of country kin to keep company with one another.

Velda watches them all, her family-by-marriage. Going in, coming out, getting into their automobiles. When Linda comes back, she takes the lead onto I-75.

Velda is proud of her only daughter doing that, driving like that. It's a little thing, a silly thing maybe, but she is proud of Linda for going on into the restroom without waiting for the aunts to walk with her. She never clutches at a pocketbook or crosses her arms over her chest; she is tough and sure like the Crandell men—well, all except for Willis. And Velda is proud of her taking off from work and keeping her teenage boys out of school. She's proud that Linda works, a paralegal at that, which sounds like she makes more money than she does. Out of all the family, Linda seems least affected by the quits and starts of Jacobs's appeals and attorney squabbles. Out of all of them, she has managed to keep up her life, work, home, children, without living for the death of Donald Jacobs, the last of the four murderers remaining. (The two buddies of the Jacobs brothers had died in prison. One in a knife fight, the other of cancer.)

"I wonder if she remembers," says Willis, keeping pace with Linda's red car, and rearranging his soft, bulky body to accommodate the sagged bucket seat.

It is almost five o'clock, but it looks later because the sun is hidden behind the clouds. Tiered, scalloped and spreading to form a seamless hull of dense gray sky.

"She remembers." It hits Velda then that he has meant does Linda remember the way to Jackson while Velda herself had been thinking about Linda and the children.

All except for Linda, the Crandells have let pity replace pride. People, strangers and neighbors, are always trying to give them money to make up for their guilt and gladness that the Jacobses and their buddies had run out of gas near the Crandell place instead of their own houses. The Crandells are famous, in Georgia especially—the most pitied. Grades are given to Velda's grandchildren in school. Most teachers give the Crandell children A's; none will give less than a B. They are shunned, the children are, for the same reason—pity. Or maybe they are shunned because their luckless taint might rub off. Next time the Jacobs gang could pay them and their families a visit. Regardless, the succeeding crops of Crandells have ceased to earn their way in the world as in the old days.

Linda's oldest boy, Dean, for example, is wearing her down with demands for the latest brand-name clothes. A Gap outlet store has moved into the Albany Mall near Sylvester. Their prices aren't much higher than Walmart and the trendy jeans and shirts are better made. Then all the kids who have to dress like the TV rich graduated from Gap to Abercrombie & Fitch. Dean is sure if he moves up, he will become part of the in-crowd, a non-Crandell. He acts as if it is his right to be rich and accomplished without ever having to *be* or *become*. Velda has pointed out to Dean that he is like a cat chasing his tail—the faster he runs, the farther away his tail gets. But the truth is, he is just as well off to keep circling with the tip of his tail ever out of reach. He is a Crandell and doomed to be pitied and shunned. The charm, the taint, is ingrained in Dean's younger brother and cousins. They take the grades given and use the pity to advantage. Velda won't live to see and doesn't want to see the outcome. One of the gifts of aging: she will be spared the results of her grown grandchildren. It comes to her like a hard wind in her face that she won't be spared, that Willis is and has been all along, a result of that very pity and compensation.

It is raining, about to storm, when the Crandells get to Jackson, and Velda thinks that it should be. Lightning gashes the bruised and swollen west sky above the all-gray compound of the prison, a series of depressing concrete and steel fortresses encased in chain-link fencing. Coils of barbwire laced through the top of the fence appear to dare the lightning and not the 130 inmates snug inside (crocheting, it's been said). Great drops of rain begin to fall, and huge humming lights from on high flood the mowed grass grounds. A beacon of light circles, spotting angular patches of rain. An American flag on a tall pole whips in the rain-driven wind, rankling a chain that sounds to Velda like an antic dog hooked to a wire clothesline.

Seated low in the idling car, listening to the rain rapping on the hood and the wipers slapping left and right, Velda keeps her eyes on the trunk of Linda's dusty red car, how the raindrops brighten the faded paint in polka dots. If she looks up she will have to see the guard checking Linda through; if she looks left she will have to see the protestors parading along the south section of fence. She will have to read their signs and mull over their messages. She can't resist it. If for no other reason than to torch the as yet smoldering hate she'll need to feel when she sees Jacobs die or not-die in a matter of minutes.

"'Murder is Murder,'" Willis reads, choking the steering wheel. "'Gas or chair, is it mercy?'" He always does that. Then repeats, "Hey, it ain't about punishment, you nuts, it's about ridding the world of Jacobs and his kind."

The guard at the gate, there to check each car through, wears an oblivious waxen face. No sign of recognition, but he knows them, he knows who they are. Velda can see him pointing out directions for parking to Linda with an arm crooked in the window and getting drenched, her nodding her auburn head to be polite—she knows where to park. In the lot of the smaller flat gray building, H-5, south of the stacked main building.

Jacobs had been put on deathwatch two days ago, meaning he was moved to a single cell away from death row. A prison staff member had been assigned to monitor his behavior. There, Jacobs had been allowed to smoke and had his own TV. For shock value, he could say all the ugly stuff unsaid in his head. He could barter locations of more dead bodies for more time.

The big deal of course, what the press always reports, is the last meal, which for some reason, Velda has begun to think of as the Last Supper of Jesus and his apostles. Last time, Jacobs had ordered a cheeseburger, fries, and chocolate ice cream and ate every crumb. They said he even licked the cream from his bowl till it shined.

Execution day, today, he had been picked up by van and taken to H-5, where he will die unless there is a stay. Five hours in the six-by-nine-foot holding cell adjacent to the death chamber. No windows, just an aluminum cot and toilet. Before, for electrocution in the chair, his head had been shaved and his right leg had been shaved below the knee, and he had been dressed in a new striped prison uniform. All for nothing. Another dress rehearsal, and him rolling his black eyes and smirking because he knew it.

Already several other cars are parked on the wet, black asphalt in front of H-5. Witnesses for the scheduled execution. When they see the procession of family cars and trucks approaching slowly along the gravel road leading from the entrance, they begin to get out, popping open brightly colored umbrellas and holding them high overhead. Some reach back inside their cars for notebooks and recording machines. Two guards in brown twill uniforms step from the doorway of H-5 and signal for the witnesses to stand aside for the family to get parked and get out and go in first.

Passing through the clanging ribbed iron gates of the compound, Velda tries to recognize at least one of the sober-faced guards posted each side of the gray walls a yard or so apart.

Hands by their sides and vacant in the face as park statues, their holstered radios, next to pistols, beep and jabber. A woman dispatcher's keen voice, thrown from the hip of one of the guards, announces trouble in lockdown in cell B. "Campbell requests assistance. All units respond."

Velda's not sure that's exactly what she hears. But she is sure another radio-thrown voice, a man's, reports that so far all is a go in H-5.

Another set of clanging iron doors, and the witnesses step from gloom to light—more hall—from radio racket and warning signs, to abrupt silence. End of the walk Jacobs had taken earlier in the day.

Inside the brief lime-green hall, leading to the death chamber and the viewing room, the only sound is the scraping and squeaking of shoe soles on the waxed white tiles, humming quiet. The building has a feel of old government clinic about it—practical and neat, hiding the shot needles and people in white to keep from shocking little children. The smell of uncured paint reminds Velda that before the walls were beige, damp-streaked with what she imagined was spit but probably wasn't. She can't bear to think what was reported to have drizzled down the walls of her bedroom while the men waited their turn to rape Mary.

Her ears buzz so that when the EXIT door opens with a warning buzz at the other end of the hall, she has trouble making a distinction between the sounds. She hopes she doesn't faint; Willis on her right is bracing her arm. Or is he holding to it to brace himself? Through the door, a prison chaplain in black enters with a black Bible under one arm. He is a tall, broad man with fine curly white hair and a cheery face held in check. He nods to the group walking behind the two guards, then disappears through another door on his left where the rushing sound of water layers the quiet.

Velda has heard, or read, that Jacobs's last act before going from his cell to the death chamber, across the hall, is the shower. More meaningless ritual, as far as she is concerned, but she supposes there has to be some order to dying, same as living. Still, the whole business, from trial to execution, seems a waste of decent people's time, emotion, and money. The new paint is a screen hiding the truth of these shamed walls.

Fifteen minutes to six and all thirty witnesses are ushered into the viewing room through a door on the left. Four varnished pine church-type pews reach side to side of the square room, walls mint-green too, fresh painted. Like a window for viewing a church baptism, after Christians took to baptizing inside, the front wall is glassed in with a shabby wine velvet curtain drawn. Velda is glad to see that it's the same curtain as before. She is glad there is a curtain to hide what's behind, if only for a few more minutes.

All gather around Velda, ever the bereaved mother and widow. Hers is a fixed and permanent role, like a queen born into her reign. Everybody seems to know Velda and her family, though the Crandells have never seen these particular newspaper people or even the guards before. They have their roles too. Roles passed down in the thirty-one years of passing.

But to Velda, only the younger Crandell children look new. Dean has been here before; she remembers him being here for the last execution-turned-stay. But was he old enough to remember? All are dressed up as for Sunday school, but here at Jackson to view a killing. Eager to be off to Denny's to celebrate or not-celebrate. But really they just love to eat; it's maybe their only pleasure. Reminds Velda of the dead Crandells, but that's about the only resemblance she can detect in this generation.

She is glad suddenly for the green paint that hides the ugly smeared walls from their tender sight. She shouldn't have let them bring the children. She can't remember why she did. Was it because it was the only vacation they'd ever known—going to Jackson? Tears leap to her tired old eyes.

Thunder roars outside. No windows looking out but there is a quick flash like lightning from a camera of the six loaded reporters crowding along the back wall.

"No picture taking," the taller guard says. He has a stiff voice, all business.

Same as at a funeral, the honored widow and her children are seated up front. A couple of state officials wander in wearing dripping all-weather coats, no hats, and their hair plastered with rain.

Members of the press mumble along the rear wall. "They say he refused his last meal," one says low. "What was it, do you know?" Somebody else says, "Not a single person here for him; I find that strange, don't you?" "They're dead by now, most of them. The rest don't want to be associated." Cool as a morgue inside.

Behind Velda, Dean is clearing his throat, sitting forward and rimming the neck of his white Polo shirt with a finger; before Velda, a newspaper woman is kneeling, whispering. She is young with bushy dark hair and a sharp nose. She smells of Witch Hazel, a remedy astringent Velda had forgotten but recalls in the form of Ned's Sunday shaved face. One of the guards spies her, is coming to ask her to leave. She has to talk fast, hazel eyes cutting left at the approaching guard.

Velda hasn't heard a word she said but knows both question and answer: How does it feel to finally get to see Jacobs die? He'll get a stay.

When the curtains part, opening in yanks, they are presented with a sidelong view of Donald Jacobs lying strapped on a narrow metal gurney. The only actor on stage, draped all in white like a play patient. A large computer monitor behind the gurney flickers and flashes blue and green symbols and the ziggy red line of his black heartbeats. Next to the monitor a compact metal machine exhibits three inverted syringes to be compressed one at a time and fed through a tube into his left arm, bandaged as if broken atop the white sheet: the first, sodium pentothal, inducing a mild state of euphoria and a muscle relaxer (easier for other drugs to get into one's system; the needle could pop out of the arm otherwise). The second syringe to be compressed by the machine contains pancuronium bromide, which paralyzes the muscles across the bottom of one's lungs, muscles that force breathing. Feels like one is holding his or her breath. The third syringe depressed will release potassium chloride to paralyze the heart. Both chemicals act in tandem to make one die.

This information of how it all works, lethal injection as opposed to the electric chair, had been sent to Velda in a typed formal letter from the State; "one" used as reference instead of "Jacobs," an unnecessary and distancing politeness. The alien chemical names had dazed her then. Now her reading voice is reciting the names in her head like facts from a tax reporting form she'd better get right.

But it is Donald Jacobs and not the "one" referred to in the letter who turns his shave-nicked head toward the window and the Crandells behind it. He is all eyes and ears with his head shaved, same as before; he looks the same, hasn't aged a bit. Velda had hoped his head wouldn't be shaved, that he would have hair like most other humans, that he would look old and haggard, or at least different. That he doesn't brings it all back too clear, from start to end.

He appears to be holding his breath. His dark blared eyes make him look shocked, but he doesn't seem scared; the even red rickracking on the monitor is proof. Maybe he is as used to playing this part as the Crandells are of his performance, or figuring like them he'll get a stay.

Velda's eyes never leave Jacobs's eyes, except to glance at the monitor and the giant old black-rimmed round clock on the wall behind the gurney that seems like an illusion of Jacobs's eyes, a third eye. The long second hand sweeps round over the numerals 11 and then 12—seven minutes till six o'clock.

Willis, seated on his mother's right, resets his imitation Rolex to synchronize with the death chamber clock (a prison guard he'd got to know on one of the trips to Jackson had sent him the watch crafted by the inmates as a money-making project). He smoothes the blond hairs on his wrist, admiring the look of the Rolex, then takes his mother's hand in his, squeezing.

The warden, in brown and brass, a bullnecked man thick across the chest, steps front and center of the window, hands clasped seriously behind. He rocks on his heels and when his lips begin to move, an oddly small voice screaks from the black-box speakers in the corners of the viewing room. "If anybody would like to leave before we proceed . . ." He leaves it at that. He doesn't say proceed with what. Then, "The attorney general is on the phone to the Board of Pardons and Parole. Checking for any last-minute stays."

He bows his head, showing a sharp side part, a stripe of white in his flossy brown hair. Then he turns, head and shoulders only, to face Donald Jacobs, whose eyes have fixed dead on Velda, or so it seems to her. Really, he's not looking at anybody, she thinks. He's just bluffing, waiting for somebody to come tell him he has gotten another stay. He looks safe, saved, behind the glass, almost Jesus-like in white. But for those eyes like bullets seen down the barrel of a gun. Used to, she worried he might break out of prison or be released and come back to Sylvester to kill her and the rest of her family and she would have to pull up this image of him behind glass for a little peace.

Four minutes to six and the chaplain seen up the hall enters with his Bible and stands next to Jacobs and mumbles a prayer— for Jacobs, not for the witnesses. Therefore, Velda feels no guilt for keeping her eyes open to see if Jacob's are closed. He only blinks, watching her. Amen. Then Jacobs rolls his head away, dismissing the chaplain.

The warden watches the chaplain leave the room, then begins speaking to Jacobs while facing the witnesses. "Donald Jeffery Jacobs, you have been ordered by the State to die by lethal injection at six PM, May the sixth, 2003, for the murders of/or participation in those of Ned Nixon Crandell, Albert Roy Crandell, Bennett Boyd Crandell, Mary Bell Hope Crandell, and Robert Dale Crandell."

He faces Jacobs again. "At this time you will have two minutes to speak to the family out there."

The clock on the wall shows two minutes to six and the second hand is swinging round.

Somebody at the rear of the viewing room whispers in breathy tones, "They say he refused the usual preacher by his side at the end. Means he's scared. Has given up using religion as a defense. He knows this is it."

"Is it true what they said about him crocheting a motorcycle?" somebody else whispers.

The warden is still waiting, glancing up at the clock.

Jacobs neither nods nor speaks. His eyes remain wide, as if taking in the last sight of the living world, these people, the Crandells, who he has doomed to a life of pity and advantage, fame.

"Say something," Velda says low.

"Mama," says Willis.

"May God have mercy on your soul, Donald Jacobs." The warden looks at the clock on the rear wall, the second hand swinging toward the 12 mark at the top and overlapping the long hand.

All hold their breath as the second hand swings over the 12. "It's good as done," Willis whispers in a choked-up voice.

Then the 1, 2, 3, 4, 5 . . .

Eyes still on his viewers, especially Velda, Jacobs's body jerks, a mere hiccup, then his eyelids blink, then close.

Nobody moves, nobody speaks. They watch before them the miracle of death wrought by death. They watch his heartbeats spike on the monitor, then redline off the screen.

Linda, on the other side of Willis, begins to cry. Dean, behind Velda, slumps over. "He's fainted," one of the aunts whispers as if she might wake Jacobs, because indeed he does look asleep.

Still, Velda watches the body before her. The curtains close in swinging snatches.

Willis sucks in air. "Was that it?" he says. Not *is* that it? Was that our life?

Velda stands weakly and walks to the window, pressing both hands and her nose to the cold glass. "You should have eat what they brung you," she says.

JANICE DAUGHARTY is the author of the story collection *Going Through the Change* and the novels *Dark of the Moon*, *Necessary Lies*, *Pawpaw Patch*, *Earl in the Yellow Shirt*, *Whistle*, and *Like a Sister*. Short stories of hers have appeared in, among many other places, *The Southern Review*, *The Georgia Review*, and *The Ontario Review*. Born in Echols County, Georgia, she married her high school sweetheart in 1963, attended Valdosta State College for two years, served as mother and wife while her children grew up, then began writing at age thirty-nine. She hasn't stopped since. Currently she is writer-in-residence at Valdosta State University.

Last Chance Son

by *Michael Morris*

Oftentimes conversion stories stop just before the real story begins. In all our lives, the moment when we are born again marks the starting line, but we are left with our entire lives to live out that new birth. "Last Chance Son" illuminates, in a comically piercing manner, what it means to begin to face the rest of your life now that salvation has been found.

—Bret Lott

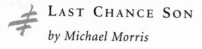

Last Chance Son
by Michael Morris

Wes Walker was still waiting for his big break when the bug job opened up. Between his sister and parents he certainly had an ample supply of career advice. His sister, Monica, had even given him one of those books about finding the color of his parachute. But Wes would be hard-pressed to know where the self-help guide had landed in the apartment among the wadded-up clothes and empty beer bottles scattered across the floor.

Mama and Daddy had told him the job with Executive Exterminator was nearing his last chance at a decent living. Daddy had said as much the last time Wes had made the trip back home to Coffee County, Georgia. "Son, nobody's gonna hire a man with a checkered application for a job with good benefits." Wes's father ripped the check for the latest rent payment out from the checkbook. "Next thing you know you'll be out there digging ditches like the Mexicans." Daddy tossed the check across the kitchen counter and motioned with his scarred thumb toward the window.

Outside just beyond the pool two Hispanic men dressed in acid washed jeans toiled in the prized flower bed that Wes's mother had designed. Last chance or not, Wes couldn't bring himself to believe that driving a Ford Ranger with a multicolored roach on the rooftop was the parachute for him.

Mother's Day morning, a day his sister called sacred, Wes lay on his so-called bed, an air mattress stacked on top of milk crates, and studied the peeling paint from a stain on the ceiling of his apartment. A brew of too much alcohol and dread crept up his throat. Another conversation with his father was anticipated the same way a toddler waits for a nurse to prime the needle for an inoculation. He predicted the scene would be a rerun of that last visit but there was no other option as Wes saw it. Monica had called the day before to make sure he would get up and meet the family for church just like they did every year for Mother's Day. Monica always was a kiss up, Wes thought. Ten years older or not, his sister wouldn't last a day in a big city like Atlanta. He had made it all by himself for nine months now. Rolling off the mattress, he could feel the carpet scrape against his bare back. So what if he had five jobs under his belt since moving here? He was meeting new people.

As proof, the people were scattered across the floor of the two-bedroom apartment he shared with an X-ray technician from Phoenix City. He kicked an empty tequila bottle across the room, barely missing a stringy red head with matching panties.

Brushing his teeth, Wes smiled thinking what his prissy sister would've thought about the party last night. He knew when he got back that afternoon a small group would still be at the apartment with the usual boxes from Dominos and Taco Bell littering the coffee table Mama had purchased. His new friends would laugh, relive the party and vote for the person "most tore up." The award ceremony was becoming a Sunday ritual.

Wes tossed water into his bloodshot eyes, gelled his hair, sniffed out a clean white shirt among those piled in the bathtub, and dismantled the diamond stud from his earlobe. With Daddy still mad about paying another months rent, Wes didn't want to further irritate him by sporting the earring. The same earring his father always addressed by lifting with a pinkie and saying, "I've a good mind to tear that thing right off."

Stepping over an obstacle course of sleeping bodies in the living room, Wes fought the chilling sweat as much as he did the temptation of his soft mattress. Outside, the smell of aged beer and fresh urine caused him to cover his mouth and move faster toward the parking lot, where he easily found the brightly painted roach that rested on top of his company truck. Putting the key into the ignition, Wes wondered for a second if the company would allow him to drive the truck out of the city limits. But deciding that was a concern someone like his sister Monica would worry about, he eased away from Piney Plantation Apartments and entered the highway of his past.

Two hours south of Atlanta the roach truck slowed to the small town speed of 25 miles per hour. Two elderly women with bright hair clutched their Bibles and crept across the street with a family of small children. At the red light, Wes felt the sting that comes with melancholy. Regardless of his reasons for fleeing, there was something familiar and comforting to him about small-town living; Like the afghan his mama would drape over him on winter afternoons.

Driving past a service station, the Dollar General store and a brick bank building, Wes grew thirsty for the town that had almost suffocated him months earlier. He had left Coffee County for a fresh start. A change of scenery is what he sought, where a few DUIs and a charge for marijuana possession would camouflage the scars of being labeled a public disappointment.

When the truck passed the large magnolia tree in front of the white steepled church, Wes saw her and in doing so felt that he had found his soul again. She was wearing a short silky gray dress with spaghetti straps the tips of her auburn hair dared to touch. Her legs were only made longer by the open-toe plat-form shoes. When she turned, her almond-shaped eyes caught his gaze and for extra measure she brushed the hair from her shoulder. Wes leaned over the wheel and smiled. She opened pink-lined lips and smiled back, tilting her head downward.

While trying to roll down the passenger window and drive all at the same time, Wes called out to her. (For an instant, the neon colored roach atop his ride and the last chance he was driving were forgotten.) He was still the Homecoming King from two years before, riding through downtown in a parade, still the one named most flirtatious, still the golden child in his family whose future had been secured with a prepaid tuition at the University of Georgia.

In a whip of his neck, it was over. He heard the screech of metal slamming into concrete before he saw the multicolored roach raining down. The roach, once proudly bouncing on the top of the truck, now lay upside down on the hood. The hood, once pristine white, was now crushed into a street meter. The right tire, like his ego, was deflated. And the long-legged creature paused, gasped, then cupped a hand over her mouth and laughed.

The man who showed up with the wrecker claimed he owned the only full-service gas station in town. ("You'd been in one natural fix if the deputy hadn't caught me.") Wes rode in Mac's burnt-orange tow truck and tolerated his advice. "Now if you had you a spare I could get her changed and you'd be on your way. As it is, I'm gonna have to patch her up. And my wife and kids are expecting me down at the restaurant. You know, with it being Mother's Day and all." The man chewed his words the same way Wes imagined he might chew roast beef. "If you don't mind waiting for me to eat with the family, I'll have you on your way soon enough."

After the man drove off in a black haze of exhaust, the bitter taste from digested liquors of assorted brands returned. He knelt by the locked gas station door and gazed at the boxes of candy tucked under the checkout counter. The chill swept over him until he rubbed his hands over the plastic trash can, wishing a fire would magically appear. Beer on liquor, never sicker.

Facing the street, Wes saw the familiar red sign standing higher than any building in town: Hardee's. A fried chicken sandwich, biggie fries and a Coke promised to be the cure. He fished for his wallet and found only a condom and a cocktail napkin with an anonymous phone number.

Wes walked across the street toward the bank and searched the sides. A teller window with a green *closed* sign stared back at him. "What kinda town don't have an ATM?" he yelled at no one in particular and at anything with living breath. A dog with burnt orange fur paused to look at him and then purposely trotted across the street. A familiar sound rolled out from the street where the dog ventured and Wes held his breath trying to make out the direction of the chimes.

They were chimes of comfort. A pied piper of popsicles and frozen Mickey Mouse–shaped ears on dog-day afternoons. Wes jogged to the front of the building and sketched out a plea to the ice cream man for a snow cone on credit.

A block away, the high-pitched sounds grew louder until

Wes turned a corner and found a blockhouse painted purple. The chimes drifted from a loud speaker attached to the top, where a TV antenna might have once been. A large white sign with stenciled black letters reading *God's Hospital* sat where a mailbox should have been. Wes walked between parked cars along the side of the street and stood in front of the small porch.

"Morning," said a woman wearing a white hat complete with a plastic pink rose. Her long white teeth shined brighter than the hat. "You best get inside before you burn alive out here in this heat. Weatherman said it would reach 92 today, and to think it's not even summer yet." The soft chimes continued to swirl in his head, tempting and inviting him to step forward. A cool trickle of sweat ran down his temple. Maybe the air conditioning would help keep the dry heaves at bay, he decided.

The woman opened the door that was patched together in spirals of colored glass. Music, cool air and the fragrance of lilac perfume rolled over Wes. A sea of black hands waved in the air. A big man whose hair seemed to have been ironed to his forehead stood on a makeshift stage, shouting and hammering his hand on a tambourine. Wes fought from laughing and cautiously leaned against the white paneled wall.

But just as he was about to turn and leave, a woman with long gray braids the texture of yarn took a seat in front of the black keyboard, and suddenly sounds of joy flung through the air. The music was almost as intoxicating as the spirits Wes had consumed the night before. Before he could help himself, he was nodding to the beat of hallelujah songs.

When the music died to a few coughs and the last remaining "Amen" was mumbled, Wes slid into a corner folding chair. "I'm just passing through," Wes had planned to respond if anyone asked questions of him. Seated next to a young girl with a comb tucked inside the back of her hair, he tried not to stare and bring more attention to himself. Not more than Wes's age, the girl smiled and bounced a wide-eyed baby on her knee.

A small man dressed in a white suit and black shirt stood behind a wooden podium. He was bald except for two patches of gray hair above each ear. The man's voice was so loud Wes first thought it was coming from the speaker attached to the outside roof. "Jesus said, 'I tell you the truth, everyone who sins is a slave to sin. Now a slave has no permanent place in the family, but a son belongs to it forever.' So if the Son sets you free, you will be free indeed."

"Glory," an older woman in front shouted and lifted an arm covered in gold bracelets.

"Free indeed. Free indeed. Thank God Almighty I am free indeed," the little man threw his head back and shouted into the microphone until the words sounded like a snarl. The big man with the tambourine jumped up again and the clanging vibrated against the walls. Wes flinched and glanced at the young girl with the baby. The infant's fearful eyes made Wes smile as if to say, *This is only make-believe, the real world will be right outside to greet you.*

"Y'all sitting out there thinking how can I be free? You're free in Jesus, that's how. I look at y'all and see how the Holy Ghost done changed you." The white-suited man, microphone in hand, stepped from the stage and paraded through the rows of people. "Done took you off dope and whiskey. Done took you from running in the streets."

As the little man made his way toward the back, a trickle of sweat and chill tackled Wes once again. The man's coal-eyed stare burned Wes deeper than a branding iron. He diverted attention by looking at the baby. The eyes were hungry and seeking. Like a wild animal in search of food, fearful of the portion offered him by man.

"People, I ain't lying to you now. That's why the sign outside say God's Hospital. We're all hurting in this world. Ain't none of us got it right. But praise God, I might not be where I ought to be but thank you Jesus I ain't where I used to be."

The woman with the white hat and pink rose jumped up and down. While the congregation clapped their hands, the electricity of excitement ejected them from the metal chairs. The screeching of metal meeting tile raged over Wes like a thunderstorm.

Wes felt his heart beating faster and a copper taste fill his mouth. Any minute the liquor would erupt in vengeance. Beer on liquor, never sicker. The words waved in his mind the same way the church people fanned their hands in the air.

The pastor took three steps and unfurled a black handkerchief to wipe his forehead. Wes nervously picked at a thread on the knee of his pants and glanced at the baby. A drop of drool ran from its open mouth while a burning sensation inched up

Wes's throat. When the pastor turned to face the other side of the room, Wes jumped at the chance. He hadn't made it five steps when the voice rang out again: "Young man, before you go, you want to share anything today?"

Wes stood frozen and dug his fingernails into the pocket of his pants. Rows of brown necks craned toward him. Tucking his head, he slightly mumbled, "I, umm . . . hit this, you know, street meter and everything. Then I just heard music so . . ."

"Speak up now. Don't be bashful. We all love you here. We been there," the pastor said in a low voice. "Young man, do you know this Jesus I been talking about?"

Wes struggled to recall the image of Jesus on the stained glassed window at St. Matthew's Episcopal and the Sunday school lessons from carefree days, now disguised in some sort of haze.

"He's the Son of God," Wes whispered.

"All right now," the woman with the white hat said.

Wes felt his cheek flinch and the chill he'd been sensing now raced the course of his spine. Faces swirled around him until he could only make out the glittering purple curtain hanging from behind the stage. "Uhh . . . I've been wandering around and everything."

"Don't you worry about none of that. Jesus ain't looking for perfection. Just looking for an open heart. He knocks, but young man, you got to step forward and open the door." The pastor stretched his arms wide and dropped his chin.

Wes eased forward and stopped. A woman coughed and an older man seated closest to Wes patted him on the arm. The white suit that the preacher wore guided him forward like a beacon. Soon hands in various textures and sizes covered his head, shoulders, and arms; hands that thawed the chill and collected the beads of sweat as he prayed the words the pastor fed him.

The bandaged truck pulled into the crowded parking lot guarded by a sign that read Julia Mae's Cafe. Wes spotted his parents' Lincoln in the usual space by the azalea bush and parked the truck behind the kitchen dumpster. The crushed side of the truck and the fender that stuck out like a snarled tooth were reminders of problems he had yet to face.

Inside, clanking forks and chatter filled the cedar-walled restaurant. Wes spotted Monica and her husband sitting at their usual corner table. "Well, hello. It's only two hours after you were supposed to be here," Monica said. Daddy sipped iced tea and grunted. Wes watched his eyes scan for the earring. Mama dangled a cigarette between her fingers. A line of gray smoke formed a silhouette around her head.

"Man, y'all not gonna believe what happened," Wes finally said, sitting in the chair closest to the window.

"Baby, thank you for the blouse you and Monica gave me." Mama crushed the cigarette in a gold ashtray and winked.

Between dispensing spoonfuls of food to her daughter, Monica smiled in that sanctimonious way Wes hated.

"Well, tell us what on earth kept you?" Mama asked.

"Got too liquored up last night?" Daddy rattled the ice in his tea glass.

As if on cue, the group laughed, Mama playfully hit Daddy on the arm and Wes shook his head. "No. Well, never mind. Now don't go off or nothing, but I sort of got in a wreck."

Mama clutched her chest and leaned forward. "Were you hurt?"

Daddy slammed the tea glass and the vibration shook the salt shaker at the center of the table. "Were you driving that bug truck? They'll fire you for sure if you wrecked that thing."

Wes looked out the window at the portable gold marquee with the words Happy Mother's Day plastered on the sides. Yellow and white balloons twirled carelessly around the sign.

"Now Hal, don't start. Baby, where did it happen?" His mother's pink acrylic nails touched his hand. The touch was warm, like the skin of the believers at God's Hospital.

"In Dawsonville. Ran into a meter post." He watched the group collectively shake their heads and then individually stare off in various directions. Monica's squealing baby broke the silence.

Daddy tucked a toothpick in the corner of his mouth. "Got a ticket, I reckon."

"No sir. A warning."

"Good, because I'm telling you right now, I'm flat not pay-ing any more—"

"But I did get saved," Wes interrupted.

The eyes at the table seemed to peer deeper than the baby

had back at the church. "What, saved?" Mama squinted, revealing cracks in the thick makeup.

"There was this black church and everything. And I heard this music so I went in. And then this preacher asked . . ."

Monica quickly covered her mouth and iced tea came out of her nose. She regained with a gale of laughter and soon led a chorus of amusement. Their laughter seemed to ring as loud as the music at God's Hospital.

Wes looked down and nervously tapped a fork against the table. He tried to laugh, too.

"Mercy me. You crazy thing." Mama's chest forced out the last reaming giggle and she wiped away a tear. "Now baby, we've eaten, but you go on and look at the menu. Hal, get that little girl to come take Wes's order."

Daddy used a menu to wave the waitress over to the table. "I'm thinking about some pecan pie. How 'bout it, Monica?" Daddy asked.

Wes pretended to study the plastic menu stained with grease and fingerprints, but his gaze settled far beyond the window. Outside, the balloons tied to the marquee danced in circles with the breeze. In a feverish fit, a yellow one twisted and turned against the May currents. With a final bow to the right, the balloon broke free and ascended higher and higher above the parking lot, eventually drifting far beyond the reach of Coffee County, Georgia.

MICHAEL MORRIS has worked as an aide to a U.S. Senator, a salesman for a pharmaceutical company, and as a public affairs manager; he began writing at age thirty-one. His first novel, *A Place Called Wiregrass*, was released in April 2002 and received the Catherine Marshall Foundation's Christy Award for Best First Novel, and his second novel, *Slow Way Home*, was named one of the best novels of 2003 by the *Atlanta Journal Constitution* and the *St. Louis Dispatch*. Morris is also the author of the novella *Live Like You Were Dying*, a finalist for the Southern Book Critics Circle Award. A graduate of Auburn University, Morris and his wife, Melanie, reside in Alabama.

The Flowers Fall

by Terry Hare

This deceptively simple story captures, in its tone and texture and subject, the kind of joyful and terrible innocence of youth, a reminiscence in which one man's folly becomes the moment through which, so many years later, he sees his value in the eyes of the truly innocent. In this way God's Word given in Isaiah 40:8 is borne out in truth: "The grass withers and the flowers fall, but the word of our God stands forever."

—Bret Lott

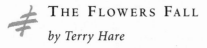

THE FLOWERS FALL
by Terry Hare

"Yes?"

The middle-aged woman peered at me through her screen door, brown eyes blinking warily behind thick-lensed glasses. Outside on her porch, the late afternoon sun beat on my neck and shoulders, coaxing the sweat from my sixty-year-old body. Occasionally I am shocked by that number. Sixty. Six decades. It doesn't seem possible.

Wasn't it just last week I was twenty-five? The vigor of youth pulsed in my veins while the follies so often accompanying it gradually fell away. I did pushups by the hundreds, ran for miles, wrote amorous sonnets for my beloved.

It couldn't have been more than a day or two ago I was forty. The challenges of work energized my life while the wounds of neglected relationships steadily accumulated. I fought for promotions, struggled through divorce, chronicled life's vagaries in my journal.

So sixty seems unbelievable . . . until I look in the mirror, that is. Then the unforgiving truth stares unblinkingly back at me, and I see the evidence clearly: tiny wrinkles around my eyes and mouth; touches of gray-white scattered throughout my otherwise dark hair; sagging lines of a body victimized by time and gravity—all of these signs of someone impaled on the stake of advancing years.

In truth, it is this number that brought me here. Or perhaps more accurately, it is the companions of sixty—regret, remorse, and the desire for reconciliation—that have ushered me to this porch on a hot July afternoon in the town of Oldport, Pennsylvania.

Oldport—the name alone conjures memories still vivid after almost five decades. The heart of my childhood was spent here, the magical years from seven to twelve when life was as simple as splashing in rippling creeks and sledding down snow-clad hills. We trick-or-treated beneath chill harvest moons, fished for bluegill in Gerardi's pond, munched apples in Schull's oak tree, hunted squirrels with slingshots, and ran barefoot over hot asphalt roads on our way to prepubescent adventures.

During the winter of '56, it snowed so much the schools closed for a week and the roads were lost in fields of drifted white. We frolicked in snow forts, drank hot chocolate by warm fires, and dreaded the day when the plows would finally condemn us anew to the drudgery of the schoolhouse.

That special winter eventually melted into verdant spring, and it was a rainy day in April 1957, when I learned something about myself.

Understand, racism was not even a concept we grappled with back then. Certainly none of us in Mrs. Gallagher's fifth-grade class at Morris Elementary gave it a second thought. True, the tremors of the coming earthquake that would define the sixties were rumbling, but those were felt mostly by the adults and went largely unnoticed by us. For lack of a worldliness that accompanies age, we simply accepted each other at face value and coexisted in naive harmony.

Not that we weren't aware of the differences between us; of course we were. But we marked the distinctions in speech and physical characteristics the same way we noticed four leaf clovers or unusual cloud formations. They merited a passing comment and were then dismissed as unimportant.

What really grabbed my attention back then were things that mattered to my eleven-year-old self: I could outrun Rodney, but not Mike. In baseball, shallow centerfield was okay when Willie was hitting, but I lived by the fence when Mike came to bat. During our football games, I didn't mind being tackled by Richie, but getting hit by Mike was like running into a brick wall.

Years later, after we had moved away, I saw Mike's picture in the back of a *Prep Sports* magazine. He had set a new Elks

County record for most all-purpose yards gained by a running back. I smiled to myself, remembering the days we had played together, and decided being second best to Mike was not too bad after all.

So I told myself through the years that what happened wasn't an issue of race; that Mike and May being black and me being white had nothing to do with it.

I still think that's mostly true, though I've seen in myself more than once the signs of bias and intolerance.

In a way, it might have been better if I could have pled racism as my excuse, for what is racism but an especially malevolent form of ignorance? Stubborn as it may be, at least ignorance can be treated with education. It's not as bad as discovering, say, an incurable defect in your character or a foundational flaw in your integrity.

May was different. All of us knew it; some of us accepted it.

May talked to herself and laughed suddenly, quietly, at unexpected times and unseen events. She was painfully shy and always alone during recess, endlessly picking flowers, weaving daisy chains, adorning her dark hair with bouquets from the field.

No one wanted to play with her, but that seemed to suit her perfectly. Her friends were the daisies and sunflowers; she hummed contentedly as she smelled their blossoms and laughed softly as she tasted the wild honeysuckle.

Of course we named her May Wildflowers; our lack of originality was complemented by our grasp of the obvious.

The pleasure she derived from her floral pursuits appeared simple yet profound, and she seemed to treasure her bouquets above all else. Indeed, the only time I ever remember May upset was when someone took her flowers; then she wept forlornly, but even this expression of pain and loss was subdued. The sight of her sitting cross-legged, slump-shouldered, crying softly into her lap was all too common.

And, since we were kids, it was also entertainment for some of us.

When baseball and football failed to hold our interest, there was always May. The fact that we'd seen her crying perhaps a hundred times already was no deterrent to causing her tears once again. It certainly wasn't new or different or exciting; yet every week one of us would make it our duty to race over to where May was sitting, crash into her quiet world, and steal the only things she seemed to care for so we could once again be amused by her suffering.

I'm happy to say I never participated in her abuse, but ashamed to admit I was too timid to prevent it until I turned eleven. I'm not exactly sure why I chose that year to grow a fledgling backbone, and no one was more surprised at this development than me.

It happened in September during our first week of the fifth grade. The boys, as usual, had split into two teams; Mike was one captain and I was the other. My team had just scored, a wobbly pass from me to Bill Zymecki.

While we celebrated in our makeshift end zone, two of Mike's frustrated teammates spotted May. She was sitting maybe twenty yards away, back to us, talking to herself while she braided daisies in her lap.

With a sudden war whoop they took off, initiating May anew into the horrors of yet another school year. I remember watching her cover her head with her hands, crying, as they snatched at her flowers, pulled at her hair, grabbed at her lap. Some of the boys around me laughed at the joke they'd seen so many times before; others averted their eyes, and still others ignored the scene completely.

Without warning or forethought I bolted, sprinting full speed toward Mike's laughing teammates. I barreled into the first one, knocking him off his feet and hard to the ground. When I turned toward the second one, he stood frozen in place, eyes bulging, mouth hanging open in midlaugh. This was an unexpected development for both of us, and I wonder now if I didn't look just as surprised as he did.

I rushed him, shouting, but before I could reach him he dropped the contraband and ran back toward Mike.

I was only vaguely aware of the silence that had fallen over the playground as I gathered up May's flowers and dropped them into her lap. I remember she cringed when I approached her, then clamped her hands over her ears as if I were about to yell at her. Instead I said simply, "Here are your flowers," and turned away.

As I walked back toward my classmates I noted their looks,

ranging from surprise to anger. The only one I really cared about, though, was Mike. After all, I had attacked his teammates, and Mike was, without question or dispute, the big dog in our little pound.

When I reached the group, it was deathly quiet, save for my labored breathing, and all eyes fell on Mike, awaiting his judgment.

After a few seconds of tense silence, he tossed me the ball and said, "You guys kick off."

And that was that. Two other times during that fall I was goaded into repeating my performance, albeit with less theatrics than the first time. In both instances, the perpetrators made only half-hearted attempts to harass May, and then only to see if I would maintain my self-appointed position of protector.

I did, perhaps more from a sense of obligation to my past actions than from any innate nobility I wished I possessed.

Obviously, I took some heat for my stance. May had been a favorite target and I had eliminated this source of fun. As a result, I endured some steady teasing. At first I didn't mind. The barbs were silly and almost always delivered with a quick smile, just to let me know their intent to rely on the "I was only kidding" defense in case I decided to retaliate. I didn't, but whenever they leaned hard on the "How's your girlfriend?" line, I was sorely tempted.

For May's part, she seemed mostly unchanged by this new order. She continued in her solitary pursuit of wildflowers, existing serenely in her insulated world. However, it slowly became clear I had made a new friend. Normally oblivious to those around her, now she occasionally directed a slow, shy smile toward me. At our in-class Christmas party, May placed a small, wrapped present on my desk.

Embarrassed, I first pretended I didn't see it, then quickly swept it inside my book bag when I thought no one was looking. Of course my classmates saw, and the sharp "Mr. and Mrs. Wildflowers" chorus ruined the rest of the party for me.

Later that night, I sullenly opened the present May had given me, and for a quiet moment its simple beauty made me forget my earlier embarrassment. It wasn't much if your yardstick is dollars and cents: only a piece of notebook paper, neatly folded into a square. But when I unfolded that piece of paper I beheld a marvelously detailed, hand drawn pencil etching of a football game.

The field I instantly recognized as our playground, and there on the sidelines sat May, cross-legged amid the tall grass, holding her precious flowers. The game itself included our usual group, but one player was drawn much bigger than the others and in much greater detail. This giant, a man among boys, was running with the ball, wading through the smaller players as if they weren't there.

The only other athlete even close to his size I recognized as Mike, his smooth, chocolate skin and muscular build handsomely and carefully drawn. But, alas, even Mike the Magnificent was no match for the Superman portrayed here by May's skilled and practiced hand.

On Superman's back was a delicately stenciled name: mine.

I was amazed. When had she ever watched us play? She always seemed so completely intent on her flowers; I never dreamed she could reproduce our games with such astounding detail. I remember staring at her gift, marveling at the time she must have invested, flattered that, in her eyes, anyway, I was the hero of the game.

But no sooner had these thoughts settled in my mind than they were chased away by the memory of my imagined humiliation. The shrill echo of my classmates' taunts burned my cheeks again, and I clenched my teeth in frustration. It was one thing to be the protector of the ridiculed; it was quite another to be joined with her in her degradation.

In a fit of childish anger I crumpled up May's gift and threw it in the trash.

By February, I was truly tired of the constant teasing and dreaded the coming of Valentine's Day. As expected, we had our usual in-class party, and as expected, May graced me with another drawing.

My classmates, of course, were delighted for the opportunity to harass me about my new girlfriend. Even Mike, normally taciturn to the extreme, elbowed me and asked how it felt to be in love. May seemed oblivious to the ruckus her unwanted attentions were causing. She continued in her slow, shy manner, smiling at me occasionally but otherwise living in her sheltered world.

I wish the story ended here.

I wish I had simply endured the year, becoming stronger for my willingness to identify with those less fortunate and maturing beyond my peers.

I wish—after all these years, I still wish—I could somehow vault back in time and relive one rainy day in April.

Another indoor recess, another day of no baseball. In a way, I almost didn't mind. Mike's team had spanked us soundly the last two times we'd played, and though revenge would be sweet, it seemed an unlikely occurrence. Frank, our tall, lanky first baseman, had moved away the week before, and Ian, our lively shortstop, was out with the mumps. Considering our current roster, a cramped and noisy indoor recess was nearly preferable to the prospect of enduring yet another loss.

Nearly, but not quite. Besides the noise and the lack of space, there was the simple fact we were often unsupervised. These were the days before metal detectors at every entrance and armed guards roaming the hallways, current-day phenomena testifying to our progress as a society.

In 1957, our teachers assumed a brief warning to behave was enough to ensure peace in their domain.

For the most part, they were right. We never burned our desks, overran the principal's office, or gambled away our milk money shooting craps in the back corner.

However, it was during one of Mrs. Gallagher's absences that Jacob broke his hand on Rodney's head for calling him a pansy. And it was during her absence this day that I broke May's heart for having the courage to share it with me.

It was nearly time for the warning bell. Andy and I had finished all the games of tic-tac-toe we cared to and then some, and I was sitting at my desk, attempting to read *Robinson Crusoe* amid the crescendoing noise.

Occasionally, it seemed the closer the clock ticked toward the end of our recess, the more frantic our efforts became at squeezing the last, precious drops of freedom from the remaining moments. Today was one of those days, and I squinted hard at the pages in an effort to block out the din of this last gasp frenzy. In five minutes, Mrs. Gallagher would make her calming entrance, but for now a kind of semicivilized anarchy held us in its sway.

Out of the corner of my eye I spotted her. For practically the entire recess she had been sitting alone at her desk, an island of tranquility in our sea of chaos. Now, however, May rose to her feet and began a slow shuffle in my direction.

I instantly tensed, fearing the worst. As my heartbeat increased, I redoubled my efforts at reading about Friday's escape from his captors. At that moment, I would have traded my birthright to join him on the pages. The closer she came, the harder I stared, as if by sheer willpower I could forestall the coming confrontation.

Still she edged forward in her slow, steady gait, and now I was no longer alone in my vigil. With every step May took, it seemed another of my classmates noticed, dropped what they were doing, and tuned in to this new form of entertainment. By the time she reached my desk, the room was silent as all eyes watched and waited. At that moment I could have slipped between the cracks in the yellow linoleum, so deep was my embarrassment.

For almost a full minute I refused to look at her while she patiently waited for some indication from me. Finally, angrily, I jerked my head from my book and glared up at her.

What I remember most about that moment is the look on her face. The transformation of her expression from quiet contentment to shocked pain took place in less than a second, yet I followed it in fascination as if watching a feature film.

If I had struck her a solid blow, the effect would have been no different. She literally staggered a half step back and gasped. No doubt she had expected—or hoped, anyway—for some sign of kindness in keeping with my previous actions on the playground. It was not in me.

Confused and upset, she stood stiffly above me for another ten seconds, then hastily dropped her present on my desk. As soon as she did, the classroom erupted with laughter and catcalls. This was the diversion they'd been hoping for, and May had delivered.

Shouts of "Here comes the bride!" and "Mr. and Mrs.

Wildflowers!" rained down on us, and I sat there, cheeks crimson with humiliation. For her part, May seemed unfazed by the persistent taunts. Perhaps she was so used to this kind of treatment that it had faded into little more than unpleasant background noise. In any event, she seemed focused on me, awaiting my reaction to her gift.

I woodenly examined what she had dropped on my desk, and for a single moment wondered how this could be. I remember glancing quickly up at her in surprise, then back at my present. As my classmates continued laughing and jeering, I slowly picked it up and held it in my hand.

A flower.

I can't honestly say I fully understood the significance of her actions at that moment. More likely, the passage of time, coupled with regular reflection on these events, have fleshed out my comprehension. However, neither can I plead total ignorance, no matter how much my conscience wishes I could.

The fact is, I knew: May had given me a part of herself.

A flower; one of her friends, one of her treasures, and she had given it to me.

I remember wondering, where did she get it? It had been raining for several days, so she hadn't picked it at recess. No, she must have brought it from home, saving it for this, her expression of love and gratitude to her protector.

Meanwhile, the taunting continued. With no clear thought other than to make it stop, I slowly rose from my chair. As every eye watched, I dropped the daisy she had given me on the floor, then ground it into a yellowish pulp with my heel.

As hoped, the jeering stopped. May's face fell, and she stumbled back to her seat. Slumping forward on her desk, she laid her head on her arms and sobbed.

I glared defiantly around the room, daring the spectators to taunt me again. As my gaze swept over them, one by one my classmates declined this unspoken challenge, returning quietly to their former activities.

All except Mike. He stood with his athlete's easy grace near the rain splashed windows, unperturbed by my little scene, arms folded casually across his muscular chest. His eyes seemed darker than usual, liquid pools of unfathomable depth.

We studied one another for a long moment, and I wondered what I saw in those inscrutable eyes. Was it criticism? Disapproval? Condemnation?

His evaluation of my character complete, he signaled our silent encounter was over with a simple nod of his head. Returning his gesture, I was suddenly overcome with fatigue and slumped in my chair, defeated.

We lurched through the rest of that day, that week, that year with no further incidents involving May and me. She continued in her isolated existence of solitary conversations with flowers of the field.

For my part, I resumed my accustomed position as second in

command of our playground troops with no apparent erosion of status or authority.

But none of us ever bothered May again.

Mike wouldn't allow it.

"Can I help you?"

I wiped the sweat from the back of my neck and nodded.

"Yes ma'am, I hope you can. I'm looking for May . . ."

As bizarre as it seems, I almost said "Wildflowers." Catching myself after the briefest hesitation, I finished with, "Wilson."

She frowned at me.

"And you are?"

I shifted my weight to my other foot and told her my name.

"She . . . she may not remember me," I added. "We were in school together many years ago, during the fifth grade."

The lady behind the screen door continued staring at me silently and I began to grow uncomfortable.

"Is May here?" I finally asked. "I promise I won't take much of her time."

After another five seconds of silence, she commanded simply, "Wait here."

When she returned, she was alone, but holding a small, cedar box.

"Can I see your driver's license, please?"

Surprised, I hesitated.

"Ma'am?"

"Your driver's license," she repeated impatiently. "I'd like to know you're really who you say you are."

I dutifully handed her my license; she examined it carefully, nodded once, then handed it back to me.

"Here," she said, opening the screen door and thrusting the cedar box in my direction. "This is for you."

Confused, I accepted the box and waited for an explanation.

"May died last year in a car accident."

She paused long enough to note the stunned look on my face.

"I'm Sharon, her older sister. While I was going through her personal effects, I found this box with your name on it."

"But I can't take this," I protested. "Surely you must want . . ."

"No," she insisted, "I know May would want you to have it. I confess I looked through its contents." She paused. "You must be a very special person."

Embarrassed by her inaccurate assessment and not knowing what else to say, I quietly thanked her and walked back to my car.

Later that night in my motel room, I examined the contents of the little cedar box with my name on it. They were simple, timeworn, elegant: a duplicate of the drawing she gave me at Christmas; a daisy pressed between two cellophane sheets; a watercolor painting of a field of wildflowers; and perhaps most disturbing, a poem, written in her fifth grader's delicate hand.

"My Friend," she had written for her title just beneath my name, "by May Wilson."

> I was lonely, scared and sad;
> Then someone came and made me glad.
> Tall and handsome, brave and true,
> Kind, bold and noble, too.
> Makes the mean ones stay away,
> Never lets them ruin my play.
> The Bible says that God above
> Gave us Faith, Hope and Love.
> Now He's blessed me with my friend!
> I will love him to the end.

Unable to sleep, I packed up the few things I'd brought with me on this failed journey of reconciliation and drove through the lonely night.

It was a long trip home.

TERRY HARE was born in Marshall, Texas, and has lived in Pennsylvania, Massachusetts, Maine, New Hampshire, Louisiana, and Michigan. At different times in his life he has worked as a general laborer, a shipper receiver, a truck driver, a roughneck, and eventually as a computer programmer. A graduate of Davenport University with a degree in business, he also graduated from Grand Rapids School of the Bible with a major in missionary aviation; he also received an AAS from Andover Business College. The father of five sons, he lives with his wife, Karen, in Wyoming, Michigan. "The Flowers Fall" is his first published story.

Turn Right, Turn Left

by Sally John

"Turn Right, Turn Left" gives us a glimpse into the complex territory that being a father and son truly is, and the way in which blessings, when we allow ourselves to examine them with the cold eye of the world, can seem to become burdens. God surprises us nonetheless with his presence and reassurance, our Father a mystery in the way He continues to turn our lives one way and another toward His will.

—Bret Lott

Turn Right, Turn Left
by Sally John

Kai walks through the back door into the kitchen.

No, I can't say my son walks anywhere. He moves like his mother, Tessie. A giraffe comes to mind. Joints scatter willy-nilly, wrenching asunder each fluid, elongated glide until—at the last possible instant before total dislocation occurs—everything reverses. Knees, hips, elbows, and shoulders flow back together again, and you know you've just witnessed a rare expression of physical grace.

The screen door slams behind Kai. He flings his arms heavenward and dances a little end-zone jig, waving a letter, his lean face split in two by a grin. His voice roars ecstasy. No words, just raw joy piercing the balmy evening.

Tessie screams and throws her arms wide. A wooden spoon sails from her hand toward the vicinity of the sink, flinging tomato sauce along the way. In two quick strides, she's prancing around with him, alternately laughing and whooping.

Chelsea and Lisbit holler and gallop over from the table they've been setting. They high-five their big brother, all the while shouting questions at him. He only laughs in answer.

From the floor, Micah steadies himself against my leg, his wet thumb tracing drool along my bare shin. He heaves his diapered bottom up and waddles on over to join the fracas. No way is he going to miss out on a group hug.

I flick off the stove burner. An excellent *penne alla bettola* is cooking. It'd be a shame to lose it. Dinners have burned during hoopla time in the Kavanaugh household.

In the instant it takes me to touch the knob, I feel myself slide into a place of warped vision. I see myself as I once saw my dad: supportive and yet . . . guarded. It has nothing to do with the *penne alla bettola*. I'm not sure I like the image.

I push my way through the group and wrap my arms around Kai's neck. My eyes well up at the sight of tears spilling from his.

"Harvard, Dad." His voice is hushed now. "Harvard!" An impossible wish has just been granted.

I don't have a voice. I can only hug him more tightly.

Kai is three inches taller than I am. His blue-green eyes carry in them the Hawaiian waters that lie at the end of the road. His hair was once the color of sunshine on a bright day when you squint until just the bright flecks dance through your eyelashes. Now, though, it's the noncolor of peach fuzz. He looks like Uncle Sam's son.

He tugs my ponytail. "Wow."

"Wow." I grin back at him. An orchestral percussion section explodes in my chest. Battle of the dueling drums. If there were buttons on my T-shirt, they'd pop across the room.

"Woo-hoo!" Tessie yells. "I knew it! I knew it! Was there ever a doubt that Harvard University would accept my son?"

Well yes, there were doubts. There *are* doubts. The kid is only seventeen. Despite his near-perfect SAT scores, he is home-schooled and he hasn't been off the Islands in eight years. His leadership skills haven't been tested beyond running a surf camp. There's still the question of whether or not a financial package exists that can lay tracks under this runaway locomotive. And he doesn't own a stitch of wool.

By the time we sit down to dinner, my jaws ache from smiling, but still I grin through the prayers. Tonight as we take our turns saying a word of thanks, Kai's news permeates. Little Micah claps his chubby hands above his head. Hoopla time.

Later, while the kids noisily clear off the table, Tessie slides onto my lap. "Congratulations, Papa."

"Congratulations, Mama."

She dabs at my beard. "Penne." Then she locks her eyes on mine.

Uh-oh. She's my best friend, and she's going to say something I'd rather not hear.

"Kit, you're holding back."

"No, I'm not." Reflex answer.

She kisses my cheek and slips to her feet. "Yes, you are."

I watch her glide toward the sink, barefoot, hips swaying beneath a long cotton skirt. Above her sleeveless blouse, wavy tendrils have escaped the pile of hair twisted under a clip. We look like remnants from the sixties, our parents' generation. We live in this simple cottage. One large room encompasses kitchen and living room. The original bedroom is at the top of a winding staircase. The kids' rooms have been added as needed, replacing the porch. We make a living by catering to tourists. Why does my son have a buzz haircut and a desire to hurdle ivy-covered walls?

Why was this desire granted?

"Hey, Dad." Kai sits down beside me and tilts his head toward the bookshelves. "You know where it all got started."

I glance at a set of old books. *The Harvard Classics.* Fifty volumes touted as the "Five-Foot Shelf of Books," encapsulating all the greats from St. Augustine to Dante to Luther to Shakespeare to Wesley. A complete liberal arts education offered to any devoted reader. I bought the used set in another lifetime.

"Not that I've read all of them," he says.

"Me neither."

"But my earliest memories are of you in that recliner, reading them."

Tears burn my eyes again. So it falls to me. I fathered him and then carved an insatiable desire into his psyche to learn by the simple act of reading in his presence a book with the name *Harvard* stamped on it.

He chucks my shoulder and untangles his limbs from the chair. "I've got to tell Grandpa."

I spend the evening in the shed working. I make didgeridoos from native bamboo and sell them to tourists. A whimsical souvenir. I figure it's the haunting tone that touches a heart chord, reminding people that while tramping through this earthly paradise, they heard a new song.

I also brood over Tessie's words and that image I had of myself in the kitchen. After a time, I turn up the CD volume and Bob Marley takes me somewhere else. Reggae therapy.

"Dad!" Kai thumps open the screen door. "Look at this! Mom just found it in the mail." He flaps an envelope under my nose. "It's for you, from Grandpa!"

"Grandpa?" My dad lives down the road.

"Check out the postmark. It's *fifteen* years old!"

"What?"

Fifteen years ago Dad lived in Omaha. The envelope feels like a dried palm leaf. It's wrinkled and has the look of something stashed out of sight for a very long time. A corner is torn and taped together. The chicken scratch is my dad's. The postmark tells me Kai was two and a half when the thing was sent.

I know exactly what I was doing when my son was two and a half.

"Weird, huh, Dad?"

"Yeah. Weird."

"Kai!" His sister's voice floats across the yard. "Telephone."

He hurries away. His world is in the now. Mine just spun backwards.

Carefully I pry open the flap and pull out a single sheet of paper. It's a letter. I skim it, blink, then start reading again, slowly this time.

I close up shop and jog two blocks to Dad's house. I find him alone on the porch, reading by lamplight.

"Kit!" He grins, of course. Grins are as plentiful as bamboo tonight. "How about that grandson of mine?"

I lean over and hug his thin shoulders, ruffle his thin white hair.

"Dad." I swallow, choking down the terror that has crept into my voice. "This arrived in the mail today. Check the date. I've never seen it before."

He scans the paper and hoots. "Whoa! Lost in some post office, no doubt. For fifteen years!"

My insides are rumbling. "How could you entrust this to the *postal system*?"

He shrugs. "I entrusted it to God. The stamped envelope was merely a vehicle."

"But if I'd read it fifteen years ago . . ." I slump onto a chair and chew the inside of my mouth.

"You know, for a while I wondered why you never mentioned it. But then . . ."

We exchange a look.

He adjusts his glasses. "'Dear Kit,'" he reads, his low voice a soothing echo from my childhood. "'Watching you struggle over there in Hawaii reminds me of the time you fell off your bike and needed twenty stitches. Seems my job is to drive you to the ER again, so here's the deal. If you move back, you've got a desk job. If you don't, that's okay too. Only you can discern between a dad's natural fears and God's best for your own family. He can do His own stitching. Now I'll butt out. With all my love.'"

We're silent for a moment.

"Dad, it has been such a long, *long* haul. If I'd seen this back then . . ." I blow out a breath.

"What? You would have spent your life behind a desk in Omaha?"

I don't know. I can't sort it out.

"Think of it this way. What do you want for Kai?"

"For Kai? What does Kai have to do with this?" I imagine my son. At the end of those lanky arms, innocence still lingers in a trace of roundness in his wrists. I hear his voice, and then I hear a day without his laughter. Like a rock slide pummeling me, the answer comes. "I want him to work with his hands alongside me and read the Harvard Classics from *home*. I want him safe from loneliness, from professors who confuse. From blue bloods who will tear him to shreds."

Dad's eyebrows rise. "That's what you want for yourself."

I cross my arms over my chest and turn away.

Dad sits silently beside me, keeping the deathwatch, as it were. I realize he's been through this already.

After a time, the stabbing pain lessens, and I can breathe. Light burns at the edge of shadows. From the depths of my being, joy oozes, a prelude to the geyser that I am certain will gush again as it has so consistently through the long, long haul. In each dying to self, there has been a painful birth of new.

"I want Kai to hear the inaudible whisper in his ear: Turn right, turn left. I want him to hear his heart beat in synch with all it was created to be."

Dad's unasked question shines in his eyes.

"No," I answer, "I never would have heard it if I'd moved back."

He smiles.

Initially inspired to write after penning a computer software manual, SALLY JOHN went on to become the author of twelve novels, including three series: *The Other Way Home, In a Heartbeat,* and *The Beach House.* In addition, she has also published nonfiction articles, speaks at workshops and conferences about writing and family issues, and is a two-time finalist for The Christy Award; writing fiction takes a backseat only to her cherished roles of wife, mom, mom-in-law, and grandma. She lives in Southern California with her husband, Tim.

The Laying Out

by Michael Olin Hitt

Grief at the loss of a loved one is a given in all our lives. And though there is the believer's comfort in Christ's promise of a room with many mansions awaiting us in heaven, when the one who is lost is a child, our faith in God's purpose and presence can be put to the most difficult test.

—BRET LOTT

THE LAYING OUT

by Michael Olin Hitt

Some boys fishing down near Athens found Hannah Marshal's body. She was caught against some driftwood. That was June of 1938.

I couldn't allow Dartha Marshal to be alone when she laid out her own daughter for the funeral. I'd always thought of Dartha as my aunt, or somebody close like that in my own family. She brung me into the church and trusted me.

I was twelve when I started following Dartha on calls for prayer or laying out the dead or whatnot. After a few years, it got to the place if Dartha showed up for prayer without me, people were asking where I was. And I started noticing that people stopped me on the street and talked about the nice weather or asked how I was. Before that, I was just another Enloe girl. Destined for no good.

In 1938, when Hannah was found, I was almost 32. By that time, I knew I'd never attract no decent man. The only man who ever looked my way was Ben Allen. He was drunk when we got married and left me as soon as I was pregnant. All I had that meant something was what Dartha taught me and the place in the church she gave me. She'd told me she saw something special in me and that God laid it on her heart to bring me into the faith.

So I stuck close to Dartha after those boys found Hannah. It was the only thing I could do.

I hate to admit it, but part of me wanted to see just how Dartha Marshal would reckon with something like this, her own daughter drowned in Laurel Creek, maybe even murdered far as we knew. I guess even this time I was looking for Dartha to teach me something.

I followed Dartha to the front door of Pritcherd's Funeral Home the day after she identified the body in Athens. Hannah had gone missing fifteen days. The whole town searched for her, some with hunting dogs, others walking in lines through cornfields or along the banks of Laurel Creek. We'd all figured out the dark truth. The last person to see Hannah was Isaac Fletcher, and they couldn't prove nothing on him. He said he loved Hannah, and he helped with the searching for her.

At Pritcherd's Funeral Home, Dartha and me tried the back door, but no one answered. Jack wasn't expecting no one, and wasn't working in the basement to hear us.

We went around front, up the steps and onto that big porch with the white pillars. Dartha wore a cotton dress and a scarf over her head, like it was a cleaning day. I'd never seen her with a scarf like that in public. After Dartha knocked, I saw Jack's outline wavering behind the leaded glass on the door. He opened the door, and Dartha's eyes filled with tears. She was holding back crying as best she could.

"They found Hannah," she said.

"I know, Dartha," Jack said. "I'm real sorry." He fiddled with his shirt sleeves, as if to roll them up. He glanced my way and nodded, and I nodded back.

"I'm wondering what you can do," Dartha said. "Make it so we can have her in the house for a homegoing."

"It's been over two weeks, hasn't it? Two weeks in Laurel Creek?"

A breeze come down along the treetops. A wind chime jingled. Jack looked down at his feet, then back at Dartha.

"There's not much can be done," he said. "Chemicals can't take away—" and he stopped.

"Maybe some kind of bag to put her in," Dartha said. "Some special casket." Dartha's voice was all business, like she was ordering groceries, but I could hear the trouble in her, like water trickling under each word.

Jack looked over our heads, toward the street. "She home?"

"They wouldn't bring her home," Dartha said. "They wanted to drive her straight here."

"That will be fine, Dartha. I'll take a look at her. See what can be done."

Dartha reached out and touched the door Jack held ajar, like she might open it farther and step in. "I'd like to be there," she said.

"I don't know you'll want that. Two weeks is a long time to be in water," he said.

"I've already seen her, Jack. I'm the one identified her."

Jack opened the door a little wider and chewed his lip. "Then you know it'll have to be a closed casket. And a larger one, too. She's probably soaked up a lot of water." Jack looked straight at Dartha. His eyes went soft. "I'll let you stay with me every step of the way, Dartha. And we'll get her home. One way or another."

"That will be fine, Jack," Dartha said. "That's very kind of you."

Only a few folks knew what it took from her—Dartha Marshal going to the front door of Jack Pritcherd's funeral home for help with her own daughter's body. Dartha had gone in the back door for years with someone's dress or suit. She was the one folks called if they wanted it both ways. To lay out their own kin and have the calling hours in Jack's parlor with the Chestnut mantel and brass lamps and lace curtains.

The fancy parlor was the problem Dartha had from the day Jack Pritcherd bought the Elliot house. "No one will want a home-going in their own living room no more," she'd said. "Not when they can have it in a mansion." We were standing across the street from the Elliot house, watching the movers carry in furniture.

"There's just something about going to a person's home to send them to the Kingdom. It'll be lost," she said. "It'll be lost."

It wasn't too many years before folks didn't call it a home-going no more. Stopped setting up all night and laying out their own kin. Except for a few. Most folks just went on to Jack Pritcherd and done it the way he said.

I don't know. Seems like to tell you how hard it was to go to Jack Pritcherd for help, I have to go way back to Eva Walters. That's how it all started between Jack and Dartha.

Jack had a set way of doing things. He'd lay out the body, schedule calling hours in his parlor, then drive the casket to the church and graveyard for the funeral.

That didn't set right with some folks. Eva Walters was okay with Jack preparing her husband Troy's body, but she wanted the wake in her house, like it'd been for her mother and brother and everyone else. Well, that's just not the way Jack Pritcherd did things. He wanted extra money for taking the casket to the house, but Dartha put a stop to that.

I went along with Dartha to Pritcherd's to see about this fee he was charging to Eva. By that time, I was always with Dartha. I guess that's when I was about sixteen, and Dartha was already past forty. She seemed like an old woman to me then. That's how young and backwards I was. I didn't know much about anything.

Dartha stood on the back steps of the Elliot house with her hands on her hips, looking up at Jack behind his screen door. "Transport," she said. "It ain't but two blocks."

"It's standard in the business, Dartha," he said. His white shirt and the whites of his eyes gleamed from behind the screen, but the rest of him was washed out by the screen and the dark kitchen behind him. "Even the trip to the cemetery has a fee," he said.

"Used to be it was an honor to help," Dartha said. "Somebody would get the body in their pickup or wagon, take it to the hardware store for the embalming. Somebody else would get the casket at McMaster's furniture. Nobody was paid nothing for transport." She squinted her eyes. "Now, you don't want people thinking you're making a profit where there used to be common decency," she said real slow, letting each word come like a little needle through that dark screen and sink into him.

After that, anyone who wanted it different from what Jack offered called on Dartha.

When my cousin, Lucille, passed on of blood cancer, I told my aunt and uncle to get Dartha. It was Dartha and me who laid out my grandma, and my Aunt Linnea didn't want Jack Pritcherd or no one but us touching Lucille's body.

Dartha came with us to the Elliot house. Dartha said we should go to the back door not the front, 'cause we was there to do the Lord's work, not to visit and have tea. When Jack opened the door, Dartha just came a-stepping in, even before Jack could get out of the way, and we followed. Linnea had a dress on a hanger. Dartha carried a special purse with make-up, hair ribbons, and whatnot.

"Dartha," Jack said. "It would be easier if you just let me do it. Just drop off the dress and I'll take care of it. They've paid for it already."

"Every conversation I have with you, Jack, is about what money you got or deserve," Dartha said. "Now, where is she? Down here?"

Jack turned on the light and led us downstairs, and there was Lucille on a metal table, a white sheet over her.

Dartha turned to Jack. "You can't have people laying out Lucille down here," she said in a whisper so my Aunt Linnea couldn't hear. "It's heartless. Heartless."

"Nobody but me's supposed to be here, Dartha. It ain't my idea."

She pulled Jack aside, and I couldn't hear what she said. Then she smiled at my aunt and said, "Jack will have Lucille upstairs in just a little bit. On a nice clean bed in one of the bedrooms. He'll bring us two basins, one of soda water, the other of camphor oil."

"Don't need camphor," Jack said. "She's been embalmed."

"And he'll bring the soda and camphor water all the same. 'Cause it's the decent thing to do. It's the smell of camphor and soda, isn't it, Linnea, lets you know it's a laying out."

And that's how it went.

Dartha had a way with laying out. She'd move real slow, like everything she done was a little prayer. Wringing out the rag.

Cleaning the body. Combing the hair. She never said nothing during a laying out. Maybe she'd recite a Psalm and say a prayer just as she got started, but that was it. She told me once that slow movement and quiet soothed the family, got them calm enough to feel God's comfort. So I learned to move slow and gentle right alongside Dartha.

The laying out for my cousin Lucille was a special one. We sung hymns while we worked and held tight to each other. Right there in Jack's funeral home.

I always figured Jack didn't mind Dartha coming to his funeral home as much as he put on. He always let Dartha have exactly what she wanted. Probably he thought it was good business. Once, in front of the post office, he said to her, "You're the link to the past, Dartha, and my funeral home is the way of the future. We make quite a team."

"I just do what's right and decent," Dartha said. She pulled my arm, and we started back toward the post office. "Team," she said under her breath to me. "If I wanted to be on *his* team, I'd be asking for money."

After Hannah's body was brung to Laurelville from the Logan County Morgue, I met Dartha at the back door of Jack's place.

"Where's Cecil?" I asked. I didn't think her husband would come along, but I figured asking about him was polite. He was a good man, always at church, never complaining when there was no dinner because Dartha was out on a call.

"He don't understand," Dartha said, and she stepped into the back door at Jack's, holding a small suitcase in her hand.

Hannah was too bloated with water for any of her own dresses, so Dartha bought a large dress at Dumm's General Store. Jack said all we could do was throw lye on her, put her in a bag and seal the coffin. No sense in dressing her. But Dartha couldn't stand the thought of it. She had to put the dress on Hannah, lay her out proper.

I could already smell her when we was walking down the basement steps. Jack untied the white bag and uncovered her. The first thing I seen was her hair, caked with mud, strands over her face. Beneath that, I saw that her face was dark and her cheek was half gone.

"Sweet Jesus," I said. It come out like a gasp before I could think about it.

Dartha looked up, her eyes filling with tears. Then she took the new dress from the bag and started putting it over Hannah's feet.

We got the dress on her, but there was no way to make it look proper. Her body was just so thick with water, there was no shape to her. She had no ankles or waist. She was thick and heavy as wet wood. Jack stood back and let us work her into the dress, from her toes and ankles up to her neck, like trying to put the skin back on a sausage. We stuffed cotton in our noses to keep off the smell as much as we could. We got her arms up the sleeves, but even so, the dress ended up not much better than a bed sheet wrapped around her. But I helped Dartha straighten it and tuck it until it looked as good as it would.

After the dress, I couldn't do no more. My stomach was turning, my head was spinning. I stood against some cabinets with Jack, thinking the dress was enough, that even it was useless, but Dartha wouldn't step away or stop. She'd brought Hannah's hairbrush and a hair comb.

It was awful to see. Hannah's eyes was gone, and part of her face—from fish, I guess, or maybe just decay—and there was Dartha, with cotton stuffed in her nose, trying to get a brush through Hannah's hair. She worked at it for quite some time before she give up, and it was the giving up made her cry hard for the first time. I tried to comfort her, but she shook me away and stopped sobbing.

Jack brung a thick canvas bag with a kind of wax coating on it. He said if we didn't put Hannah in it, the smell would come right through the casket. Jack and I were the ones who put her in. Dartha stood there. Her face was white. Her eyes didn't blink.

"I'll get her in the casket and bring her home," Jack said.

Dartha stood like she didn't hear anything Jack said.

"I'll do the rest, Dartha," he said.

"C'mon, now," I said. And I pulled at her arm until she followed.

She walked home without saying a word. Usually, when we was walking is when she talked most, telling me why she done what she done. She'd tell me why she began with confession before going on to healing, or why a poultice of catnip tea and beadwood bark was good for blood poisoning. Or why the Lord works through nature before through miracle. That sort of thing. But on this day, there wasn't nothing to say. Dartha's face was blank, and she didn't look to either side but just kept going straight down the sidewalk. I hadn't learned nothing that day except the ways we normally done things don't always bring no comfort or peace. That was about it. And I didn't see nothing I could do to help.

Cecil was readying up the house when we come in. He'd cleared a place for the casket in the living room. When he saw me and Dartha come through the door, he took Dartha in his arms. She sobbed for a spell, and he eased her down on the davenport.

"You could have spared yourself that," Cecil said. "Some things it's best to let others do," he said.

She stopped crying and glared at him. "Well, it's done," she said. "No sense in arguing anymore."

"That's right," I said. "We done the best anyone could ask."

We waited a long spell for Jack to bring the casket. We just sat in quiet together. Wasn't nothing to say. It was like we'd already started the wake, even before the body was brung. And I got to thinking about my own losses. Not just my grandma, but my baby that was stillborn. Dartha helped me in the delivery. She wrapped him, then got the minister for a baptism. My baby was just a little thing, but looked ready to be born. Perfect, except he never took air in his lungs so his skin was pretty dark. And Dartha sat with me for hours. Just sat with me. Held me when I cried, but mostly just sat in quiet.

And when I didn't come to church the next Sunday, she come to my house, and read me Psalm 77. I still have it to memory.

> *I cried unto God with my voice,*
> *even unto God with my voice; and he gave ear unto me.*
> *In the day of my trouble I sought the Lord:*
> *My sore ran in the night, and ceased not:*
> *my soul refused to be comforted.*
> *I remembered God, and was troubled:*
> *I complained, and my spirit was overwhelmed.*
> *Thou holdest my eyes waking:*
> *I am so troubled I cannot speak . . .*

It was just how I was feeling. There wasn't no comfort. But the Psalm goes on, and strength is found in the memory of God's good works. Dartha had come to my house to tell me it's the memory of His works gets us through the dark times. And just her coming made all the difference.

Hannah's casket was delivered in a black hearse. Jack and three of his nephews put a stand in the living room, then brung the casket in the house, and Cecil helped, too. It looked real heavy.

The casket was awful big in that living room. Took up most of the room. After leaving space for people to sit on the davenport, there was hardly room for chairs along the wall. Jack left, and the three of us stood, staring at the long, dark wood of the casket.

"She's with the Lord," Cecil said. "These last two weeks, she's been with the Lord. I guess there's comfort in that."

"Comfort," Dartha said. "No comfort in any of it."

"All things work for good," I said. "For those who love the Lord. It's hard to see it now, but we have to trust."

"Don't quote me scriptures," Dartha said.

I thought of the way Dartha had come to my house after my baby died, how she read Psalm 77 to me. I took up her Bible from the end table and thumbed toward the Psalms. I was going to read her that Psalm, remind her that some pain can't be comforted. "Suffering has to have a purpose, even when it hurts so bad," I said. I thumbed through the pages. "Just think of our Lord on the cross."

"Our Lord," Dartha said. She swatted the Bible out of my hands. It hit the floor and slid to the wall. Its pages fluttered open. "When His friend Lazarus died, He raised him up. He wept for a moment, then brought Lazarus back. And His own death," she said. "I'd rather be on the cross nine hours than lose my child. Physical pain's nothing. Nothing like thinking of your girl in the dark water, struggling for air, churning in the current."

My eyes was fixed on the Bible, laying open next to the front door casement. I glanced up at Cecil. His eyes were wide.

"It's God that will get us through this, Dartha," he said. "God and each other."

"What does God know about pain like this? When His Son died, he knew why. God knew *why*."

Dartha's chin shook, but not with crying. It was something else raging in her. Her lips pursed. She glared at the casket.

"For the first time, I wish I was Catholic," she said. "I'd pray to the Mother of Jesus. She knows. She knows." Her hands went a-shaking. "The Father and the Son," she said. "If I didn't need the Holy Spirit so bad, I'd forsake them all."

"Now, Dartha, you're upset," Cecil said. "You don't know what you're saying."

"I know exactly what I'm saying. I could hardly recognize her. And now look at this. It's no way to send her home."

Her chin began to quiver, but this time with crying. She fell to the floor. "Sweet Jesus," she said. "Sweet, sweet Jesus."

I did what she done for me. I sat next to her, so close her sobs shook me, her tears dotted my dress. I kept quiet. I knew it wasn't the time for nothing but this. I remembered her sitting with me after my baby died. And I figured out what she already knew. The words and the Psalms come later. Much, much later. Now was the time for movements, slow and gentle.

I put my arms around her, and I let her words be the ones that hung in the air, like a cry in the dark. *Jesus. Sweet, sweet Jesus.*

MICHAEL OLIN HITT is Professor of English at Mount Union College in Alliance, Ohio, where he teaches fiction writing, American Literature and Native American Literature. He has published stories in *The Notre Dame Review, The Nebraska Review, Puerto del Sol, The Other Side*, and *Windhover*. He has also published a book of literary nonfiction and prayer wisdom called *The Word of God upon My Lips*.

The New Church

by Bret Lott

The author of this story hopes that "The New Church" tells the story of one young man's discovery of what true fellowship means, and along the way a redefinition of the term family *in its most complex, important, and spiritually rewarding form.*

THE NEW CHURCH

by Bret Lott

Of course Robert wanted to sell his car, but there was something about selling it to a pastor that made him want to step back a minute, rethink the whole thing.

The man put his hands on the steering wheel again, looked down at the passenger seat beside him, then touched at the buttons on the radio. He said, "I'd want to take it for a drive, a little test drive," and ran his hand along the dashboard, touched the steering wheel again. Then the man turned, looked up from where he sat to Robert here in the parking lot of the Albertson's he'd just merchandised, the ninth stop on his sales route today.

Robert was a Christian himself, had been born again a little over a year before, so it wasn't that he was afraid of the man, or that he didn't trust him. He was a *brother*, so what was it? Why was he weirded out over this, a matter of sales, one brother to another brother in Christ?

"A test drive. No problem," Robert said, and smiled at the

man. "Exactly right," he said, "a test drive," and heard how his words fumbled out of him for whatever strange reason they did. Why was this so hard, talking to a pastor about selling his car, when Robert himself was a salesman, did this stuff all day long? He felt himself smiling too hard at the man, felt himself nodding and smiling still harder, and he looked at the car, imagined already, five minutes into the deal, what might happen when the man took it out for this test drive. He wondered if there were anything he knew of that could go wrong and reveal to a pastor that the car he was being sold was a dog.

But it was a good car—he'd taken care of it, changed the oil regularly, washed it every other Saturday whether it needed it or not. It had never broken down, never been in a wreck, and now, faced with selling it to a pastor and with the prospect of having to let the man drive it around, a man of the *cloth*, he suddenly couldn't name why he wanted to sell it. It was a perfectly good car. Perfectly good. Maybe he ought to keep it after all.

He probably could have guessed the man was a pastor even if the man hadn't brought it up. Robert had just finished filling the shelves at the Albertson's with six-packs and twelve-packs and two-liter bottles of RC and Mug Root Beer and Schweppes mixers, then had filled out the orders for what to ship in the next day to fill the holes left in the backroom.

Then he'd come out to the parking lot to find a man in a black suit and white shirt peering in his driver's side window, both hands cupped to the glass.

"What do you think?" Robert had said, his voice all smiles and truth and *sales*, same as every time he spoke to a store manager about an end cap display or side stack he wanted to sell. Here was somebody looking at his car, the one he wanted to sell, and the fact he was a salesman seemed suddenly an unexpected blessing: he'd use his skills from the job to get rid of his car. Of course he would. He was a *salesman*.

The man had turned from the window, surprised for a moment, the look on his face—the open mouth, the eyebrows up—more a kid caught at something than a store manager he was about to present a buy-in.

But the man recovered just as quickly, smiled, crossed his arms. He had gray hair—Robert figured he was around fifty or so—and was thin and had on old-fashioned wire-frame glasses. Before Robert could even put out his hand to shake, the man said, "Saw your sticker." He'd taken a step back then, nodded at the car.

Robert had thought he was talking about the FOR SALE sign with his phone number and how much he wanted—$1900 for a two-year-old Datsun B210—taped in the window behind the driver's seat. But then he saw the man wasn't looking at the sign, but at the rear window, and Robert had looked too, had seen the fish sticker centered there at the bottom of the window, the word MARANATHA inside the two intersecting lines. He'd put the sticker on back there not but a week or so after he'd been saved.

"Yep," Robert had said. "I'm a believer," he'd said, and heard how odd that was to say out here in an Albertson's parking lot. *I'm a believer*—wasn't that an old Monkees song?

The man had nodded, smiled, waited a few seconds before he'd said, "I'm a pastor." He'd nodded once more, and Robert nodded too—so much nodding, he thought, over a car and a sticker and being a Christian. But then the words the man had said came to him: *I'm a pastor.*

Now here they were, talking about a test drive, and Robert, for whatever reason he could not name, felt his stomach knot up.

The pastor climbed out of the driver's seat, smiled at Robert as he stood. "Don't have the time right now to drive it. But maybe you could come over tonight to my church and we can take it out."

The man crossed his arms again, tilted his chin in a way not at all unlike a store manager sizing up an offer, and Robert looked past him to the sticker. For a moment he wondered how much money off what he was asking for the car a pastor might want from a believer. A brother in Christ.

And of course, in the next moment, he was sorry for that, the cynicism of it, the judging of this man as wanting to get the best deal he could on a car because he was a pastor—that was what he'd called himself, *a pastor*; not *a Christian*, not *a believer*— and because the one selling the car was a fellow Christian. That was a sin, he knew. It was a sin to assign this man he didn't know that ulterior motive, banking on a better deal because he was dealing with a brother.

He looked back at the man, and at the coat and black tie, the white shirt. The uniform of a pastor, Robert thought. Not much different at all from that of a manager.

He looked down from the man then, and saw the shiny black tips of his steel-toed shoes, and here were his navy blue pants, the light blue dress shirt, the navy blue tie with the swirly RC logo at its tip: the uniform of a salesman.

Maybe it was a sin, thinking this guy was after a deal. Or maybe Robert was just being careful. Maybe it wasn't a sin at all, he thought, to be wary.

But he wanted to sell the car. He *needed* to sell the car. And he was a salesman. That was what he did. He could do this. He could.

Robert crossed his own arms then so that he held his route sales book across his chest. "What time would be good for me to come by?" he asked, and opened the route book, pulled from his shirt pocket his pen to write down directions. He smiled, nodded one more time.

The problem was that he owed more on the car than it was worth. Sure, it was a good car, got him where he wanted to go and hadn't yet given him any problems. But every time he climbed in, which meant fifteen or twenty times a day all day long, store after store after store, there was this element of his life that nagged at him: he owed more than the thing was worth.

He pulled out of the Albertson's parking lot once he'd filled in his route sales order in the binder, the directions to the man's church up in Garden Grove tucked into the sleeve inside the back cover, then turned right and headed up Brookhurst toward Von's, his next stop. He had eight more stores to get to before he would have to head in, post his sales, replenish the merchandising paraphernalia he kept in the trunk and backseat—all the bottle hangers and carton stuffers and shelf strips and corbuff and oddball pieces of paper everywhere inside the car—and he wondered if the pastor might have thought the car was a wreck for how sloppy the inside was, and wondered, too, if the man might ask for even less because the inside looked like a sty.

He stopped at the light at Brookhurst and Adams, and glanced down at the passenger side, then over his shoulder at the backseat: it was all work stuff, the things one would carry doing the job he did. Messy, but just stuff. There wasn't even a Burger King cup or a Naugle's wrapper anywhere around. If the guy was going to ask for less because Robert had a job, he thought, then let him. He wasn't going to budge off the price. Not a cent.

But he would have to clear it out, vacuum the thing, wash it again tonight before he met the man at his church at a quarter to six. Which meant he'd have to get in early to the office in Lynwood, which meant he'd have to cut short the merchandising at a few stops, which meant he'd have to order more than would necessarily fit into the backroom, or just bite the bullet and order less than the store needed.

And here he was, counting the cost.

He spent the rest of the day thinking about all this as he went store to store, leaving off bottle hangers at the Von's and carton stuffers at the Stater Brothers on Harbor Boulevard, fronting six-packs of cans on the shelves at the Ralph's on Adams and doing the same with Schweppes mixers at his second Albertsons, the one on Fairview, all in an effort to finish the route early enough to allow him to clean the car before he let the pastor test-drive it.

Counting the cost was a phrase he'd heard a lot about in the year since he'd been saved, especially in the College and Career Wednesday night Bible study meetings he'd been going to. It meant, of course, that you had to think about things before you jumped into them, that there were unforeseeable moments and lines and angles to things that could add up to more than you had bargained for to begin with. But it also meant the opposite of that, he'd learned as well: things that seemed more than you could afford could also be free, a paradox certainly, but one that held weight when he measured it against what Christ had done for him, how He'd given up His own life so that Robert could accept the gift of his own new life for free.

The College and Career meetings were at different people's houses, depending on which week it was—he and his room-mates' house was the third Wednesday of the month—and were taught by a guy maybe five years older than Robert who was an assistant pastor at the church. Everyone in the group was a member of First Baptist Church of Huntington Beach/Fountain

Valley, and was about the same age, some still in college, some starting out their lives either with or without it. There were about twenty of them altogether, and they were friends, hung out together, went to movies, concerts, went backpacking together and out to dinner. They were a community, and when Robert had begun to attend the church only a few weeks after he'd been saved, he'd been welcomed in without a thought, as far as he could tell, from anyone.

The teacher, Rick, had a thin fumanchu mustache, wore John Denver glasses, and was a newlywed, his beaming wife, Betsy, with her Dorothy Hamill haircut sitting beside him at every meeting and putting in her own take on things whenever she saw fit, though never in a way that stopped the flow of thought and word and prayer going on. Then, after teaching and that prayer time, which sometimes took a half hour or more, everyone who felt so moved praying out loud by turns for each other, the group would go out to the garage or backyard or wherever there was room enough to mess around, play touch football in the field at Newland Elementary behind Aaron's house, shoot pool in the common room at Eileen's apartment complex, listen to records at Don's, or just talk.

They were good people, he had come to see. The same people he had always known at any point in his life: just kids, whether they had been in trouble with drugs or the law or with parents or school or with anyone they met. They all had had their problems—their sins—and most every one of them continued to work on how they could live now that they were saved. There was Nicki, who had been kicked out of her house when she was fourteen by her mom and her boyfriend and had been homeless for a time in Santa Ana and who now worked at the Coco's at Fashion Island while she took classes at Golden West; there was Don, a brainiac who'd just graduated from UC Irvine with a degree in chemistry and whose parents were so wealthy he hadn't yet any plans to work; and Jason, who sometimes showed up to Sunday mornings and Wednesday nights smelling of the alcohol he swore he'd quit drinking months before.

And there were his housemates, the three other guys he was renting the place on Tullow with: Jeff, the one who had grown to be his best friend for how easy it was to talk to him, a surfer majoring in art on the seven-year plan at Cal State Fullerton and who was a janitor nights at Sowers Middle School so that he could surf in the afternoon; Phelan—no one ever called him by his first name, Ken—who was from Illinois and enrolled at Fuller Seminary, a prematurely bald kid who freely drank from the case of RCs Robert brought home from work each week but who also marked the level on milk cartons and cereal boxes so that he could tell whether the other three had been in his food, a move that never kept any of them from freely partaking of his Cheerios; and Tom, another surfer but more a musician, a full-time music major at Cal State Long Beach—the same commuter college Robert had graduated from last year—who led the Wednesday night group in songs before study time and who sang at the weddings that picked off another one or two of the group every few months.

They were all a family, finally. That was what Robert had come to see in the year since he'd been saved and had started attending this church and these Wednesday night meetings, and in the months he'd been living with these friends of his. They were blood relations, bound together despite all their varied histories by the one moment in each of their stories when they reckoned themselves with God. It was what they shared, that most intimate moment out of anyone's life when you saw the chasm between yourself and *Logos*—between your futile life and True Meaning— and saw that chasm deeply enough to give up your life, and in grace go forward with a purpose.

It was sin that bound them together, the acknowledgment by them all of its presence in their lives, but more importantly their freedom from it that made them family, though that freedom from it meant the battle grew even more fierce as they plunged ever deeper into their lives living in this newfound grace: it seemed that at some point every Wednesday night, once the teaching and prayer were over and that time of messing around had begun, that one or another of them could be found with Rick or Betsy—the guys with Rick, the girls with Betsy—somewhere alone and talking, tears spilled in the kitchen by Nicki or Eileen or Laura, Betsy carefully touching the girl's shoulder as she quietly cried; Rick outside, leaned against the hood of somebody's car inside the halo from a streetlamp, beside him Aaron or Chris or Jeff or even Robert himself, arms crossed or on their hips, and talking quietly, ending always with a prayer, while others in the group carried on with the joy of a family gathered midweek to be together.

Counting the cost was big with Rick, and the notion of sin washed clean by Christ serving as both high priest and sacrifice at once was a cost beyond measuring, beyond our fully understanding. And yet sin still wore at them all, the cost of giving one's life up to Christ still a miracle with each day they lived. Sometimes it was a ragged miracle, other times a bright and shining surprise. But it was a miracle all the same.

Because Robert had his sins, knew them as intimately as anything anyone could ever know, sins gone over time and again and yet again in the same way one picks at a scab or savors however briefly, the bright copper taste of blood in the mouth after a punch. He'd had sex with his girlfriend for the last two years of college, a girl who summarily dumped him when he was born again, afraid, she'd told him when she'd said it was over, that he would become a Jesus freak; there was his hatred and envy of his older brother, a cocaine addict who'd lived a life as profligate as one could imagine, and who was still, while in rehab, his parents' adored child; and there were his parents themselves, who had brought him and his brother to church their entire lives but had done so, Robert believed, only because it was what one did. His parents' lives, then, seemed hollow to him, his father warning him over Sunday afternoon dinners not to let this Jesus stuff get in the way of his job at RC and that even a fish sticker in the back window of a car he drove on the route was inappropriate, his mother changing the subject to Robert's brother as soon as her husband opened his mouth about God or Jesus or sin or grace.

He'd moved out three months after he'd been born again, in him no measure, as far as he could tell, of anger at his parents; rather, Jeff and Tim had asked him one Sunday morning if he wanted to share a house, and Phelan had been sitting one row behind them and leaned in, said, "If we make it four, it'll cost that much less," and now here they all were. He'd felt as he'd moved out of his parents' house, his life condensed to a duffel bag, a suitcase, and a cardboard box packed with photos and the few books he hadn't sold back when he was in college, a kind of relief and release. His parents were away in Santa Barbara visiting his brother and he could leave them to him. He was getting on with his life, trying to trace out its pattern before him by simply moving forward into it.

And though he had come to know through those talks with Rick that he'd sold his parents short, that they were better people than he'd believed them to be, knew as well that his resentment of his brother had to do with the fact his parents had no choice but to tend to him, and that his brother had problems that might somehow be helped more by a brother who loved him than one who held him at a remove; had come to know too that the relation he'd had with his girlfriend was something that could not be erased, and that God would have the right person for him, someone who would understand and forgive him, when He saw fit to have that person arrive— though he had been shown all this, prayed over and around and through it all, still the sin that lingered most fully and that was perhaps the most killing kind, a sin that squashed the Spirit flat each time Robert let it out, was this creeping cynicism he had known all his life, manifest this day in seeing the pastor as a schemer. The cynicism in him permeated most everything, from his seeing momentarily in the kids huddled with Rick or Betsy a kind of drama uncalled for, though he himself had had meetings like theirs; and it was there in his choosing to empty Phelan's milk carton in order, he rationalized, to teach him a lesson; and it was the sin of cynicism that kept him from telling his brother he loved him, as that would play into the whole scenario his brother had painted himself into and from which he gathered so much love from their parents.

It was cynicism Robert felt was his deepest sin, his darkest facet, the one he returned to because it was familiar and on the surface harmless: this was all in his head, and nowhere else. But it was a sin nonetheless, an element of his life that kept him from being as close to God as God desired.

And now maybe that was what was bothering him most, Robert thought as he made his way off the 605 into Lynwood and to the office to post his sales, the stores called on, the sales tallied. What was the cost of *cynicism?* he wanted to know.

Already the pastor had caused him to lose sales because Robert hadn't merchandised as he should; who knew, too, what the store managers would have to say if and when customers began to ask for product from the backroom because the shelves were empty?

How did you count the cost of being a cynic?

And as soon as he'd put the car in park outside the dull yellow office on Paramount Boulevard, Robert here an hour early and facing the wrath of his supervisor Lynn who would grill him no end as to why he wasn't still out on the route, he knew the cost was this: looking at a pastor he did not know from a church he did not attend as though he were out to nail him, give him the shaft, buy his car for as cheaply as a *pastor* could from a *believer*.

Here was sin.

He'd hoped to talk to Jeff when he got home to the Tullow house. Today was Tuesday, Rick and Betsy and the meeting tomorrow night, so he wouldn't be able to ask them about this quandary, if indeed it were even that. He wanted to talk about this whole thing, this business of business between believers, and wanted too to talk about his doubting of the pastor's motives, and this sin he knew was his own. But neither Jeff's VW van nor Tim's station wagon were in the drive. Instead, there had been only Phelan's green Galaxy 500.

He and Jeff talked about most everything, Robert sometimes staying up until Jeff got home from Sowers on Mondays or Thursdays or Fridays so that he could ask him about matters he'd read of in the Bible, or to talk about the girls Robert had begun to date, or just about work, the nature of sales and how Robert had to deal daily in a kind of lie, talking managers into buying product day in and day out that no one really needed to drink. Or Jeff would want to talk about his classes, or a pot he had thrown that had cracked in the firing, or about Carla and the on-again, off-again plans to get married one day. Jeff was hypoglycemic and had to make sure he'd eaten enough or his words would wander off into some uncharted world, his sentences as curled and breaking as a wave he'd have no chance of riding, and so Robert would have to sit and watch Jeff eat a bowl of cereal at one in the morning before they could get started. He talked to Tim less so, the other surfer in the house tuned in to his music and chords on his acoustic guitar too often to let Robert's cares enter. But it wasn't to Phelan he would ever repair, his being enrolled in seminary a trump card he played too often for any of them.

Robert parked behind Phelan's Ford, and climbed out, popped open the trunk. He'd clear space back here first to make room for all the junk inside the car, and as he loosened his tie and slipped it off, wadded it up and stuffed it in his pocket, he wondered if he'd even have time to change out of his uniform before he'd have to be at the church. He bent to the open trunk, gathered up a scattered stack of carton stuffers, bounced the bottom edge of them on the bumper to try and straighten them before settling them inside the cardboard case he kept back there for the point-of-purchase material. After this he'd have to wrestle the vacuum out here, then wash the thing, dry it, maybe even Armor All the tires and dash before—

"Roast beef in the hands of an angry God," he heard then from the house, and Robert glanced up from the trunk to see Phelan push open the screen door and step onto the porch, a half sandwich in one hand, in the other a bottle of RC. Here was Phelan's bald head, his mouth moving with food, like always. He was tall and skinny, and was forever mysteriously tan for someone who ostensibly spent as many hours as he did at the books. He made it to the car, stood off to Robert's left just watching and chewing. He took a swig of RC, another bite of the sandwich. Tuna salad, Robert could smell. Phelan's favorite.

"What do you mean by that?" Robert asked, and reached into the trunk, pulled out the unfurled roll of corbuff, started at rerolling it. "This isn't about the milk again, is it?" he asked, and glanced at him, gave a small smile, the kind he hoped might get him going just for the fun of it.

"Come on," Phelan said. "Jonathan Edwards? You've heard of him, right?"

"Sure," he said, and here was a lie. A sin. But this was Phelan showing off, and this sort of cynicism wasn't anything other than a joke. At least that was what Robert told himself.

"It's a joke up at Fuller, in the deli place in the cafeteria up there," Phelan said, and took another bite of the sandwich. He had on flip-flops, Robert could see, though he complained bitterly every time he wore them about how hard it was to get his toes to hold them onto his foot, this inability even to wear flip-flops further proof, Tim and Jeff and Robert always hooted, of his being from Illinois. "It's a sandwich they make up there and sell at the deli counter." He swallowed, swigged at the RC while Robert tucked the corbuff roll in the wheel well, then picked up dozens of shelf strips, the one-inch by six-inch pieces of plastic printed with the names and logos of different brands that popped into the shelf and which littered the bottom of the trunk. "You get it, right?" Phelan asked, and leaned his head one way, waiting for an answer. "They call this one sandwich the 'Jonathan Edwards Roast Beef in the Hands of an Angry God.'"

"Yeah," Robert said. "It's a joke," he said, and found a rubber band in the cardboard box, wrapped it around the shelf strips.

"You don't get it," Phelan said.

"I guess I don't," Robert said, and tried at the smile again, shook his head. He settled the shelf strips in the box, then reached farther back into the trunk, pulled out the feather duster back there, and the price marker, and two rolls of Day-glo orange 99¢ stickers, set them in the cardboard box.

"So what's wrong?" Phelan asked then, and the question caught Robert, the honesty in it, and the charge behind it: Phelan, the one of his roommates he was quickest to discount, saw there was something in him he needed to talk about.

231

Robert stopped, looked over the open trunk lid to the house, to its dull beige stucco, to the two windows—his bedroom was the window on the left—and to the screen door closed shut. Suddenly the place seemed like an implacable face, the door its mouth, the windows its eyes, the dull asphalt shingles and the peaked roof its hair, a face that held in it the secret of what a family really was, and one that wouldn't divulge it. A Southern California version of the face of God.

Here was Phelan, delivered to him from inside the home they shared to ask this sharp and open question that could only be answered by the truth of Robert's cynicism, its residence in his heart still, and its resonance in everything he saw.

He turned to Phelan then, put a hand to the trunk lid, pulled it down until it shut. "You want to know?"

Phelan took another bite. Somehow, he made the smelliest tuna sandwiches in the world. "I've got ears to hear," he said. "And I'm listening."

Robert looked at him. He blinked, took in a breath.

"I've got somebody who may be interested in the car," he said, and leaned against the rear fender. "A pastor. He told me that's what he was before anything else, and he wants to test-drive it, and there's something about the whole thing that makes me wonder about—"

"Don't do it," Phelan cut in, and swallowed. "Don't. I'd rather have a nonbeliever buy my car than a believer any day of the week." He took a quick bite at the sandwich, chewed as though the food in his mouth were on fire. Suddenly he was on, worked up, and he pointed at Robert with the hand holding the RC, jabbed the air so that the carbonation sizzled up and almost broke over the bottle brim. "Or fix my TV, or fix my toilet or my car or sell me one too. It's because there's this kind of implied trust thing going on between the two parties, a kind of wink-wink thing going on, that means one of you is daring the other one to do inferior work or charge a lower price or whatever because you're Christians, and you can trust each other." He snatched at the sandwich, the food still a fire in his mouth as he spoke, wadded up tuna salad in there spinning faster than his words. "But what happens when something goes wrong?" he went on, and jabbed the bottle at him again. "Then you're not supposed to sue each other, right? First Corinthians six, verse seven: 'Now therefore there is utterly a fault among you, because ye go to law one with another. Why do ye not rather take wrong? Why do ye not rather suffer yourselves to be defrauded?' Yeah, the Christian plumber who sticks it to you for three hundred bucks for a water heater that bursts the first week'll trot that old line out and you'll be screwed. Because there's also Proverbs ten, verse ten you have to deal with, 'He that winketh with the eye causeth sorrow: but a prating fool shall fall.' Professor Schmidt in my Ethics course says that there's this new thing going on, the Christian Yellow Pages, and that the whole thing is a kind of wink, or sort of, because of this whole—"

"Thanks," Robert said, though the word came out small and

a little frightened of what he had unleashed. He nodded, turned from leaning against the fender and maybe too quickly opened the car door to start clearing out the inside, and suddenly he felt his face hot for the words from Phelan, the fire of them, but also the truth of it. Because wasn't this what he had thought himself all along? Didn't he fear being taken precisely because the words from the pastor identifying himself as being a pastor meant some kind of wink, as Phelan and the full import of his Fuller tuition seemed to be screaming through a tuna salad sandwich?

And he thought of his own cynicism, and how it paled to nothing beside Phelan's chapter-and-verse version.

Still, there were the verses. There was the truth of them.

"Christian ethics looks like this topic you can understand, Schmidt says, but it's really not possible to grasp," Phelan went on, a specter behind Robert, an angel and demon at once, he thought, a family member vomited from the mouth of a beige stucco house in Huntington Beach, California, by a God who seemed only bent on making things murkier for him.

He pulled right off Euclid and into the church parking lot, maybe a dozen other cars here, and he wondered at that, all these cars on a Tuesday evening, and he parked. Just as he'd feared, he hadn't had time to change out of the uniform, and could only make the best of things by looking in the rearview mirror to straighten the tie he'd put on while driving over here, center the knot at his throat. He scanned the inside of the car one last time—he'd actually gotten the dash Armor Alled, even with Phelan hanging around and preaching the whole time about the state of the "capital C Church," pausing only once to go back in the house and reemerge a minute later with another bottle of RC—and Robert nodded to himself. The car was clean, sharp, inside and out. Worth the $1,900 he wouldn't come down from for anything.

He climbed out, dusted off his knees one last time, the material there left at the end of every day with the sheerest clouds of gray for his having spent so much time kneeling to the shelves and merchandising.

Then he looked up at the church, wondering where the pastor was, and again what all these cars might be for. The lot was about the same size as the one at his church, room for maybe a hundred cars or so, and he saw that the church itself didn't look a whole lot different from his own too. This one was older, sure, the trees around it bigger, the asphalt of the lot a bit more cracked. But it was the same stucco as his own, had the same A-frame end that fronted on the street, and was circled by the same concrete sidewalks. A church, he saw. Only that.

And now here came the pastor from inside the brown double doors up at the front of the building, him still in his own uniform of that black suit and tie, that white shirt, and in the second or two it took for the door to close behind him, Robert saw a few people in the foyer in there.

The pastor was smiling as he stepped off the sidewalk toward Robert, and glanced to his right, toward the street. Robert looked too, saw a car pulling in, behind it another, and here was one more slowing down out on Euclid, settling itself in the small line suddenly out front of the church.

Now here was the pastor, and Robert smiled, put out his hand. The man took it with both his hands, shook it hard, and winked.

Robert felt himself blink twice in a row.

"Listen," the pastor said, and let go Robert's hand, put his hands to his hips. He looked to his right again and the cars, then to Robert. "Listen," he said again, and smiled. "I hope you don't mind, but there just isn't enough time tonight before the service. I thought I'd have a little more time than this, but it looks like I won't be able to until after the service." He looked down at the ground, then at the cars coming in, then Robert again. He smiled. "I hope you'll forgive me. And maybe we can get this done after the service." He paused. "If you want to come to the service, that is. Of course you're welcome."

"Service?" Robert said, and put his hands in his pockets, felt himself rock back a little on his heels.

"It's our second night," the pastor said, and nodded toward the street, where another car was on its way in, "and I just thought for some reason there'd be more time before we got started."

Robert looked out to the cars again too, and only now did he see the canvas sign stretched sideways across what must have been the church's eye-level billboard out on the street, across the sign the words *Revival Monday–Thursday*, beneath it, in smaller letters, *Guest Preacher Rev. James LaRue.*

How had he missed that?

"Well," Robert said, and here was the flush of heat to his face for whatever reason. Maybe it was that wink, he thought. Or maybe the prospect of a revival. Or maybe it was the whole thing, the scam this seemed suddenly on him: get somebody you didn't know to come to your revival by telling him you'd test-drive the car he had for sale.

The pastor had actually *winked* at him.

"I'm a believer," Robert said, the words out of him not the confession he'd made to this man this morning, but suddenly the same kind of dare, Robert believed, that the words *I'm a pastor* had been from him there in the Albertson's parking lot.

He nodded, smiled, and started toward the church door before the pastor could say another word.

But for all the cars it seemed were out in the lot, there weren't as many people inside as he'd thought there would be. He walked through the narrow foyer, nodded at the knot of four or five women there; in with them was a girl about his age, cute with brown hair down to her shoulders. All of them nodded back to him, but it was the girl who smiled at him, said, "Welcome," to which Robert said, "Thank you," and stepped through the open double doors into the sanctuary itself.

He took a seat in the next to last row of the sanctuary, a room that could hold maybe two hundred altogether, same as his church not twenty minutes from here, and watched as a thin string of people came in behind him, settled themselves in closer to the front, all the while talking to each other, touching and smiling. From where he sat he counted twenty-seven people, including himself and the pastor, who went from person to person, smiling again and again, shaking hands again and again. The pastor hadn't introduced him to anyone, but then Robert, he had to admit, hadn't allowed him to, had only made straight for those double doors, and into this pew.

Then here came up the aisle in the middle of the sanctuary a man in a blue pin-stripe suit, a sharp shock of gray hair shellacked into place atop his head. He was as tanned as Phelan and stood a good six inches taller than the pastor, who smiled solicitously at him once he'd made it to the front of the sanctuary. The pastor then shook this Reverend LaRue's hand with both of his, and Robert took in a deep breath, settled as deeply into the pew as he could. Who knew how long this would take, he thought. But he was here to sell the car. He might, he thought right then, even wink at the pastor once he'd handed him the keys for the test drive.

The room went silent, of course, and the pastor took the pulpit, smiled and nodded to the small crowd. He put both hands in his back pockets, cleared his throat, said, "Thanks for everyone coming back tonight. And for those who weren't here last night, God bless you for coming," and he nodded at Robert, all the way back here in the next to last row.

Robert nodded, gave a small wave back.

The evening went from there: the pastor led them in a couple of hymns from the hymnals in the back of the pew, a woman suddenly at the piano to the right of the pulpit playing just as well as Mrs. Pasley did at his own church; then came the pastor's introduction of the reverend—Jimmy, he called him—and how he was still the pastor of a church out in Bakersfield, same as he was at last night's introduction, and how he was still a lifelong friend of the pastor's from their days together in seminary, to which a few of the people gathered laughed.

And then the man took the pulpit.

In four hours, once the service will be over and the test drive too—the pastor will tell Robert he doesn't want the car after all, that his daughter, the cute girl with hair down to her shoulders, wants a 280Z instead—and after Robert will have driven his B210 from Seal Beach to San Clemente twice, PCH all the way, he will park in the driveway behind Jeff's VW van, and make his way quietly through the darkened house back toward Jeff's room, because Robert will see through the half-open door at the end of the hallway that his light is on in there. Robert will want to tell Jeff what has happened, the amazing thing at this church he's never been to before, the awesome moment that has made selling the car something that doesn't matter at all, and that has made his time spent driving up and down the coast the joy it has been, and he will push open Jeff's door, allow himself in, only to see Jeff propped up in bed. He will be snoring, asleep sitting up, and in one hand he will hold a spoon, in the other a tipped-over bowl of Grape Nuts, the cereal and milk spilled down the front of Jeff's T-shirt and the sheet around him. Jeff will have fallen asleep in the middle of his meal, and the thing will be so funny that Robert doesn't have the heart to wake him, and he will close the door behind him, climb into his own bed, and lie awake for another hour, just watching the sky out his bedroom window, the one to the left of the front door of a house that looks all the world like a house, and only that. Not God at all.

And on a Thursday night three months later, a drunken sailor driving his Camaro will slam into Robert's car in the driveway of the Tullow house. Robert will be safe inside, listening to a Vince Guaraldi record with Tim and Phelan, and the sudden sound of metal ruptured into metal will jar all three from the couch and chair, and a moment later Jeff will rush into the house from the garage where he has been throwing a pot at the wheel in there, his hands washed with clay to his elbows, to tell them *There's been a crash, there's been a crash!* And while they are waiting for the police to arrive, he and Jeff and Tim and Phelan will huddle with the drunken sailor—there won't be a scratch on him—in the front room of their house, and they will pray with this sailor, talk to him about Christ; Robert will even give him his Bible, and this will be the only thing the police will let the man bring with him once they cuff him and carefully place him in the back of the squad car. The car will be totaled, leaving Robert with $300 still owed on it. But he will pay it, and be glad to have done with owing more than the car was worth.

Five months from now, Phelan will come home from Fuller to announce to the Wednesday night group that he is dropping out of seminary and wants to be a dentist.

On a Sunday morning eleven months away, Kay, a girl from New Jersey and Eileen's best friend from childhood, will walk into the College and Career class, and when Robert sees her laugh for the first time, sees the way she leans her head back, her hair falling off her shoulders just so, and when he sees the ease with which she lets go this joy in her, hears the song of her voice—for it is a song, doesn't everyone hear that song?—Robert will be startled beyond his imagination at her, a girl like no other he has ever met, brought to him precisely as God sees fit; a year later they will be married.

Two weeks after that, Jeff and Carla will get married, too, and Tim will have sung at both their weddings.

Three years after this night at a revival, Robert will be in graduate school and studying to be a writer, his skills as a salesman finally coming into play in a way that will matter to him; he and Kay will be living in the western Massachusetts town where Jonathan Edwards lived when he wrote "Sinners in the Hands of an Angry God."

And thirty years hence—who can say how these things happen? And who can understand the hand of God, His plots and inventions, outside of living them day to day to day?—Robert will have become a Famous Novelist, and somehow, somehow, he will for a while be living and teaching in Jerusalem—yes, Jerusalem— where he will be a guest in God's HQ, and on a Sunday morning in January, the air outside cold and crisp and blue, he will be inside Jerusalem Baptist Church with his wife of twenty-eight years. It will be a humble church, the congregation small for such an important city, maybe only thirty people in the chapel with its sound system that sometimes works, sometimes doesn't, and with its heater that observes the same schedule. He will be sitting in a chair in the third row, the same place he sits each Sunday for the few months he is here, and he will be listening to the Special Music, for so it is called in the program he will be holding in his hand.

There will be five singers up in the front of the chapel, an Israeli woman his own age next to a Nigerian man a little older than his older son in the Army—their younger son will be a junior in college—next to a Korean man who stands beside two Filipino women, all of them behind a Scottish woman playing the piano. The array of nationalities he will see is something that will bear no remark, as the congregation itself will come from around the world: the service leader will be a Welshman, the woman who makes the announcements each Sunday from Holland, the man who prays over the offering each Sunday a Russian.

But the moment that will bear remarking is this one, right

now, thirty years hence, when the hymn begins, the five up there beginning to sing.

They will be terrible. They will start out flat, will grow flatter with each verse of the hymn—"And Can It Be"—and, as though to make matters worse, the pianist, the lovely Scottish lady who wears her hair up in a bun and a skirt made of her family's tartan every Sunday, will, as she does every tune she will ever play, get every ninth or eleventh or sixth note wrong, until by the last words of the song—*Bold I approach the eternal throne, and claim the crown, through Christ my own!*—it will be all Robert can do not to wince visibly for the pain of this sound.

But then, in the way only God can arrange the synapses of the brain, a network placed in order to deliver Robert to this moment long before he was ever born, he will remember that evening of a revival, and it will be as a blessing to him, because he will hear in this noise these people make, and in the clumsy play of the fingers at the piano, the beauty of Christ, revealed only through what he had found that night in Garden Grove.

I am not worthy of your blessings, oh God, he will pray right there and then, in a chapel in Jerusalem. *Never have I been worthy of your blessings, nor will I ever be. But I accept them, and pray I will not forget them,* he will pray, and decide then too to try and write a story about this all, if only he can be blessed enough by God to get himself out of the way of himself, so that he might set down the right words, and only those.

Because only after the forgettable sermon by Reverend Jimmy

LaRue, Robert in the next to last row and aching to sell the hell out of that car now that this was almost over, this scheme by the pastor to fill the pews if only by a one of a kind of sales job he'd bitten on hook line and sinker; and only after the altar call in which no one went forward; and only after the pastor had come back to the pulpit, stood again with his hands in his back pockets, did the story begin.

"Do we have any prayer requests?" he said, and reached a hand from a pocket, adjusted his glasses.

That was when it began.

The story had nothing to do with the sermon, and would have nothing to do with the car and the pastor's words about his daughter wanting a 280Z instead, once he returned from the test drive. It had nothing to do with Robert's father and his warnings about Jesus and grace and MARANATHA fish stickers on the car he drove on the job, and nothing to do with that brother of his in rehab and the doting mother, his very own mom. And it had nothing to do with a girl he had had sex with believing it to have been love, and it had nothing to do with the fact, finally, that the reason he wanted to sell the car was because he'd bought it planning to ask her to marry him, the car itself become a kind of symbol every time he climbed in of the stability he had foreseen in a career with RC Cola, a kind of stability he had planned to bring into the marriage he would ask her to enter into with him, only to have her tell him she was afraid he would become a Jesus freak, now that he had been saved.

And the story had nothing at all to do with even the moment of his being saved, and the rally he'd attended for no good reason other than that a classmate in the Business Ethics class he was in his last semester of college had asked him to come along that night to hear the man. He was a famous apologist, the classmate told him, though the man was no one Robert had ever heard of. And the story had nothing to do with what he had heard there that evening, the utter sense and logic and evidence that had ushered him into an understanding that he'd really had no idea who this Jesus was all along, even though he'd been baptized at fourteen because it was what one did in the church he'd attended back then, and the story had nothing to do with his sudden certainty that Jesus was indeed who He said He was, and had nothing to do as well with what he'd written on the index card he, like everyone in the auditorium, had been passed once the apologist's talk was over: *I want to know more*, he'd written, and then his phone number.

The story had nothing to do with the phone call he'd gotten a week later from his classmate, the one who'd invited him and, it turned out, was working with the college group that had sponsored the visit; it had nothing to do, either, with their meeting for coffee, and the talk that followed, and that resulted in Robert's praying one night alone in his room, the same room he'd grown up in and that he'd lived in through his years at a commuter college and would live in until he moved out to the Tullow house a few months later, a prayer that cut to the bone his sense of self, a prayer of surrender and loss, and a prayer of arrival into a place he had never been before, and which brimmed with hope, a deep hope he had never felt before, because he knew that through that prayer he had found Truth and Meaning, and through that prayer he had crossed the chasm between his own futile life and over into that Truth and Meaning. A prayer he could not describe for the failure of words in the entire matter, but a prayer bound up in words, and that meant the beginning of new words, a new life, a new *logos*.

The story had nothing to do with any of that, nor did it have anything to do with that classmate, a guy named Aaron who went to this great church over in Fountain Valley that Robert ought to come and try out one Sunday.

"Any prayer requests?" the story began, and a woman in the third row stood.

She had on a purple dress, her gray hair in a bun exactly like the Scottish woman at the piano will wear thirty years from now, and said, "Jerry's brother is dying. He's forty-one, and we just found out this morning he's got pancreatic cancer."

He saw the pastor pull a piece of paper out of his back pocket, saw him pull from inside that black suit jacket a pen, and write something down. But then he stopped, looked over the rim of those glasses he wore.

"What's his name, Janice? Your brother-in-law," he asked, and nodded to her.

"Michael," the woman said, and sat down.

It was exactly what Rick did at prayer time every Wednesday night: write it down, ask for the details that mattered.

A man in a green plaid flannel shirt stood up, and the pastor said, "Bill?"

"I got a man out to the job site today who got his foot run over by a bobcat," he said. "It's broken in fifteen places, and he's going to be out at least two months. Three kids, and, well," and here he paused, looked down; all Robert could see was his back, his head disappearing as he bowed it. "Well," he said again, quieter now, "this prayer is for him and me both, because I don't have any workman's comp on him and I don't know how I'm going to be able to help him out."

"We'll do what we can, Bill," the pastor said, and wrote on the paper.

There were more prayers, the story starting up in earnest now: "My son in the Coast Guard." "Scott and his girlfriend. That's all I can say." "My grandma out in Florida has got pneumonia." "My daughter needs to know Christ."

They were garden-variety prayers, Robert saw. Of course they were. But he saw more than this, suddenly and fully: they were *words* one to another, needs worked out in *words* by these people, same as the words he and the family he knew on Wednesday nights used to make known their own prayers. All of them garden-variety needs, just as the prayers he needed for how he felt about his dad, and about his mom, and about his brother, and especially, he began only then to see—for here was the real story, the true story—just as the prayer he needed to extinguish his own cynicism were all garden-variety prayers.

But they were *his* prayers. This was *his* story, these were *his* words, and he saw, finally, what it meant to pray, and felt in the same moment a kind of scraping free, a kind of scab lifting to lay bare fresh new skin beneath.

These were the words that came to him, the image he saw of his heart and the feel of the cynic in him beginning to leave.

Here was a family. It wasn't his family, not the friends he played touch football or shot pool with, and this pastor wasn't a man he'd stood leaning against the hood of a car beneath the halo of a streetlamp to tell of how he felt about his brother, or the girl, or his father and mother. But it was a family.

And then the pastor folded up the piece of paper, placed it in his back pocket, stepped down from the pulpit. Once he was down on the floor of the sanctuary, he put his hands out to either side of him, his fingers splayed and held out flat, like a paper doll or an Egyptian hieroglyph, Robert thought for an instant, and now people up there were standing, moving together, he could see, and now—*Oh no*, the cynic spoke, *not that, not that*, though the voice seemed somehow to grow more faint with each word—they were beginning to hold hands, every one of them, and now the pastor looked up at Robert, nodded. He smiled, said, "This is how we close our services, and you're welcome to join us," but Robert found that he was already standing, that he was already, right now, out in the center aisle, the same one Jimmy LaRue had walked up and that he didn't want to find himself on, but here he was, walking it and freely so until suddenly, suddenly he was holding hands with two people, one the man whose worker had broken his foot in fifteen places, the other the woman in the purple dress whose hair he will recognize one day.

They smile at one another, this group congealing into a circle of sorts around the first two rows of pews in this sanctuary of a church he has never been to before, and the pastor says, "Let's pray."

Then these people speak, this family he does not know. But he is listening, he is listening.

And at first these are strangers he hears. These are prayers about and for people, he believes for one last breath out, that he doesn't know; these are prayers for a family, the cynic lets him think in one last dim cry, that isn't his family.

They're not yours, he hears, but he's not even sure those are the words he has heard, the sound of these prayers drowning out in joy and sorrow the cynic, though he fears perhaps that voice is only hovering and just beyond what he can hear.

But now, even now, now: in among these people around him, in among these prayers, he hears it, he hears it: here is a voice he knows.

Eileen's, he hears. But not hers alone. Because now here is Don's, and now Nicki's and Aaron's and Chris's, and here are Laura's and Jason's voices too, and here too are Rick's and Betsy's, and everyone else in the Wednesday night family, and of course Jeff's, and Tim's, and Phelan's too.

Because they are all one.

And now there are others here, too, he can feel, people he doesn't know, and can't yet see: a girl with a laugh like a song, and two boys, one in the Army and the other in college, but boys at the same time; and somewhere out there is a woman at a piano she plays too beautifully for the keys to accept, and now he hears other music—how can he ever tell this to Jeff, or to anyone, and what does Wednesday night even mean, when every night is available for these moments, these words, this music?— now he hears music, hears voices singing off-key and perfect, warming a chapel in a holy city, he somehow knows, with their sound, their gift, their words.

And now, feebly, carefully, in fear and trembling, he joins them all, this family, himself one among them, and prays.

I am not worthy of your blessings, oh God, he prays right there and then, in the sanctuary of a church he has never been to before. *Never have I been worthy of your blessings, nor will I ever be. But I accept them, and pray I will not forget them,* he prays.

BRET LOTT is the author of eleven books, most recently the story collection *The Difference Between Women and Men* and the nonfiction collection *Before We Get Started, A Practical Memoir of the Writer's Life*. He is writer in residence and professor of English at the College of Charleston, and lives in Mount Pleasant, South Carolina, with his wife, Melanie.

Ithaca

By Kelcey Parker

In this disarmingly moving story, which takes its structural lead from the seventeenth chapter of James Joyce's Ulysses, *we see the story of faith—in self, in God, and in faith itself—worked out against the fact of our own impending mortality; the story's sense of play, borne out by its structure, gives us an awareness of the inherent surprise we encounter at the way God's hand can work in our lives.*

—Bret Lott

ITHACA

By Kelcey Parker

"Alone, what did Bloom feel?

The cold of interstellar space, thousands of degrees below the
freezing point or the absolute zero of Fahrenheit, Centigrade
or Réamur: the incipient intimations of proximate dawn."

—James Joyce, *Ulysses*

*What parallel courses did Leonard and Sammy Two follow prior
to meeting?*

Leonard: having gone to his doctor for the investigation and
treatment of various pains and discharges, had performed upon
him a great number of tests and probes with large machines
bearing the General Electric logo, and was, ultimately, diag-
nosed with terminal colorectal cancer.

Sammy Two: having recently been born, was, with his siblings—one male, one female—occupying a nest constructed
carefully by his parents at the meeting point of several branches,

upwards of one hundred feet in the air, when a bolt of lightning struck the primary branch, causing limb and nest to fall to the ground, killing mother and siblings, and leaving Sammy Two, unable to feed self or move on own, resting in a small circle of grass, in shock and facing certain death.

But the two courses did not remain parallel, but turned inward and intersected, as the two met very soon after?
Indeed.

Then the courses were never, in fact, parallel?
Correct. By definition, parallel lines will never intersect.

Provide the scientific classification of Leonard and Sammy Two.

	LEONARD	SAMMY TWO
KINGDOM:	Animal	Animal
PHYLUM:	Chordate	Chordate
CLASS:	Mammal	Mammal
ORDER:	Primates	Rodentia
FAMILY:	Hominidae	Sciuridae
GENUS:	Homo	Sciurus
SPECIES:	Sapiens	Carolinensis
SCIENTIFIC NAME:	Homo Sapiens	Sciurus Carolinensis
COMMON NAME:	Human Being	Eastern Gray Squirrel

What did Leonard do, and what was done to Sammy Two, following the perceived reality of imminent death?

Leonard said to his doctor, with bravado: "Mark my words. The Lord will heal me and you'll have a medical miracle on your hands."

Sammy Two was very nearly killed a second time.

Did Leonard's words to his doctor accurately reflect his belief in the possibility of a miracle?

Leonard was, for his years, a big, strong man, who believed in a God even bigger and stronger than he. He absolutely believed God *could* do it, though he was less certain, since the quiet nonevent that was Y2K, that God actually *would* do it. For on the eve of the millennium, he had stayed up with Betty, watching Dick Clark and the pagans in Times Square partying like it was 1999, as it were, and waiting for the ball to drop—and not merely literally.

He was prepared. He had water, paper products, canned goods, candles, kerosene, even a generator, stored in the basement in boxes labeled A through Z, then AA through HH. He was prepared for the Lord to usher in the new millennium with fire and without electric power. As a Christian, he had learned about God's wrath. As a Cornell student, he had learned Emersonian self-reliance. As a Big Red football player, he had learned to fight, to be prepared. And prepared he was. But, as everyone knows, nothing happened. Computers did not suddenly believe it was the year 1900 and self-destruct or accidentally launch any missiles. The worst thing that happened was a few bad hangovers. Y2K left Leonard feeling like he was suited and psyched up for a game that was cancelled because the other team's bus broke down.

His first instinct following the cancer diagnosis, if we're truthful, was to tell the doctor he was going to battle it out with the cancer himself—and win. He would outsmart it and out-health it, so to speak. Instead, he offered up his illness as a challenge to God Himself.

What was Leonard's particular view regarding the apocalypse?

The one in which God kicks the greatest amount of you-know-what: dispensational premillennialism. When trumpets sound, like they did for the Big Red team at Cornell, Christians will be raptured, meeting Christ in the air. During the seven-year period of great tribulation, Christians will be judged and assigned places in the forthcoming millennial kingdom. Then follows the battle of Armageddon—a battle better than the Rose Bowl (where no Ivy League teams ever made it anyway)—culminating in the thousand-year reign of Christ in the New Jerusalem, as announced by the seventh trumpet and foretold in the book of Revelation. Verse 11:15.

How did Sammy Two almost die a second time?

After surviving the major fall, Sammy Two was very nearly crushed under the seventy-five-pound pressure of Josie Lambert's foot. It was the first warm, but also wet, day of March, and Josie and her brother Lou were playing outdoors after school. As they raced through the backyard, Josie, catching a mid-stride glimpse of a gray-brown blob in the spot where her sneaker was sure to land, and thinking it a dog turd, extended her foot just enough to avoid contact, and succeeded in landing just beyond him. Getting the attention of her brother for reenaction and inspection, Josie found that it was not poop but something that would have been even worse to land on. "Daaaaaddddd," she cried, and Dad found Sammy Two (not yet so dubbed), and, within fifteen feet, his dead sister, and, thirty feet away, under the branch he planned to move that day, Sammy Two's dead mother and brother.

Why did Mr. Lambert say, "Well, I'll be a suck-egg mule," and why did he immediately think to bring the squirrel to Leonard Anderson?

Though he knows not what it means or where he first heard it, Mr. Lambert often employs said phrase in moments of disbelief and general amazement. Mr. Lambert, who has often tuned out of his neighbor Anderson's enthusiastic explanations and interpretations of the Book of Revelation and the imminent coming of the Lord Jesus Christ, recalls hearing him say one thing that interested him: that several years ago Mr. Leonard Anderson raised a baby squirrel that answered to the name of Sammy.

How did Leonard's second wife, Betty, handle the arrival of Sammy Two?

With her usual social grace and strong presence of mind. She dried her tears before opening the door and called to Leonard to retrieve Mr. Lambert's squirrel when all she wanted to do was slam the door in Lambert's face and say that Leonard was busy saving (or losing) his own life and could not, just now, be bothered. She smiled and thanked Mr. Lambert for Leonard, who, instantly dazzled and filled with purpose, withdrew the tiny squirrel from the hand towel that Lambert held him in, said, "His little toes will get caught in the threads—best to use a handkerchief," and retreated to the kitchen with his new project and prize.

What happened to Leonard's first wife?

She died.

How did he meet Betty?

Betty lived seven houses away. Her husband had also died, a year prior, and she prepared a casserole for Leonard, who ate one cheesy, chickeny, creamy piece alone every night for nine nights after the funeral, and on night ten, the casserole pan was empty but his heart was full. When he returned the clean casserole pan to Betty—whom, it should be noted, he had known for many years as a very fine neighbor—Leonard also brought along a marriage proposal.

How did this go over with Leonard's two adult daughters?

Not well. Not well at all.

Why did the arrival of Sammy Two not go over well with Betty?

Because Betty knew her husband. Before the doorbell rang, they had been sitting at the kitchen table, making plans for Leonard's healing/treatment. Leonard held Betty's hand, squeezing her fingers too hard against her wedding ring, and prayed; on a piece of paper he drafted a list of phone numbers for the prayer chain. Betty composed a list of foods for Leonard's new diet; she created a schedule that balanced her work with Leonard's transportation to and from the hospital. (Leonard was retired and collecting barely a pittance; Betty, a few years younger, continued her job as receptionist for a local dentist.) Betty was angry, for she had lost her first husband to cancer, and it seemed absolutely like Leonard's God to strike her twice. When the doorbell rang, she learned that He had struck thrice: lightning hit the Lambert's branch and here was a baby squirrel.

Why did Betty think but not say a certain scatological term?

Because Leonard didn't like it when she cursed, and she tried not to when he was around.

What did Leonard think and/or say in his first moments with Sammy Two?

He said, like man on the sixth day of creation: "I'll call him Sammy Two." He thought (with no little relief or gratitude): This is a sign from God who has heard my prayers. He said: "Betty, where's the heat lamp?" He thought: Sammy Two must be just a couple weeks old because his ears weren't opened yet.

What, then, did he not think to think?

He did not think to think that perhaps God was giving him Sammy Two as a bit of joy *in lieu of* the healing miracle. Betty, on the other hand, was very tuned in to this potential and particular irony.

Describe Sammy Two's condition upon entering into Leonard's care.

Sammy Two was in generally good health, considering. Leonard was immediately concerned about his body temperature, which seemed to be lower than it should be, so the heat lamp was found and shone upon Sammy Two. Leonard was secondarily concerned with a tiny cut on Sammy Two's belly. He treated it with diluted hydrogen peroxide, which he dabbed with a cotton swab, and then with a spot of Neosporin. Leonard was thirdly concerned with getting food into Sammy Two's belly. Leonard fumbled about the kitchen and bathroom medicine cabinets, searching for his medicine dropper (Betty followed behind, putting everything he removed back into place), then he concocted a solution of sugar, salt, and warm water, which he fed as delicately as his large hands would allow, into Sammy Two's hungry mouth. Leonard was fourthly concerned with Sammy Two's elimination. He stroked the squirrel's genitals (he was officially a boy!) in order to stimulate the flow of waste and was rewarded with a dirtied tissue.

Having tended to Sammy Two's physical needs, what did Leonard do?

He cleared the scattered crossword puzzles and remote controls from the table next to his recliner, and he set the heat lamp there. He settled into the recliner, holding Sammy Two in his hand, and stared at the little walruslike face with its whiskers and sepia-colored body no bigger than his thumb, and he stroked, as gently as he could with the knuckle of his index finger, the velvety body that pumped and breathed in soft, rapid pulses. He turned on *The McLaughlin Group*. He forgot, for the first time all week, that he was dying.

What did Betty do?

What she always did when anything, including her job, her children, and both of her husbands, disappointed her: she imagined the ideal. Even as a teenager, she had a very strict sense of how high school, for example, *should* be: all lettermen sweaters and pom-poms. Now she could scarcely distinguish between her actual school experiences and the ones she had conjured in her mind. Between the vague lives her son and daughter were living in faraway states and the lives she had envisioned for them. Between the heroic death of her first husband, Ted, and his actual, unpleasant decline.

Leonard had always had a habit of talking about two things around the neighborhood: Jesus Christ and Cornell University. She totally tuned out the former, but, even when both of their spouses were alive, she found herself drawn to his bravura regarding the latter. He'd played football, pledged a fraternity, written for the sports section of the school paper. He'd been wild, virile, young. She hadn't known him then, of course, but she was attracted to who he said he was, and she thought of this person a lot. She found herself looking through his college yearbooks, trying to merge the two disparate images of Leonard into one.

Betty, then, retreated to the bedroom, leaving Leonard and Sammy Two before the television, and allowed herself to forget her concerns about money and health insurance, about death and disease, and to get lost in thoughts of Leonard: young, strong, successful, healthy.

What did Leonard and Sammy Two do all day while Betty was at work?

They became the best of friends. They got on famously. Sammy Two grew quickly, thriving under Leonard's care, and Leonard took great pleasure in studying Sammy Two's personality. Sammy Two, for example, took tissues straight from the box and stored them on the floor behind the couch. Leonard thought this very smart and funny of him. Betty, less amused, cleaned up the tissues. But Sammy Two would grow very distraught when his tissues were not where he had placed them and made clicking and scolding noises at Betty until she left his tissues alone.

They played football. Leonard would tuck an acorn into his palm, holding it with his thumb, then use his middle and index fingers to run across the kitchen table toward the end zone. Sammy Two proved himself to be an excellent safety—always making the tackle in the nick of time and causing a fumble that he recovered himself. Leonard taught Sammy Two the Cornell fight song.

During a nice string of warm April days, Leonard thought of what fun it would be to take Sammy Two out, show him off a bit. So he came up with alliterative errands: milk at Meijer, window washing fluid at Walgreen's, birdseed at Bigg's. Leonard put on his spring jacket, and Sammy Two hopped on his shoulder and crawled down inside the sleeve. At the checkout counters, Leonard would make a little click sound, and Sammy Two would pop out on cue to the delight of all. *What the? Is that a squirrel? Hey Pete, check this out!* It was a hoot.

What did Leonard and Sammy Two not do?

Remember doctor appointments.

What did Leonard do the time he saw a dead squirrel in the road as he drove home?

By this time, Sammy was moving freely between the house, where he slept, and the birdhouse, where he took his girlfriend. Leonard could not remember if Sammy was inside or not when he left. He pulled in the driveway and bolted from the car—leaving the door open to *ding ding ding*—and ran to the backyard (slipping on the hill beside the house, hurting his tailbone and soaking his pants through to his butt) where he whistled furiously, frantically, *Sammy where are you,* then again, *tweet,* scanning the birdhouse, the trees, the wire, until, oh thank You, Jesus: Sammy.

Fast-forward a couple of months.

June arrives, and Leonard has undergone a number of treatments, thanks to Betty who monitors him like a child, and no thanks to his daughters who are unable, even after four years, to accept the presence of Betty in his life. Nothing else has happened. The cancer does not seem to have spread, but it is not going away either. His 18 to 24 month timetable has reduced to 15 to 21 months. His squirrel will outlive him.

It is time for the annual family reunion at Maple Run, the cottage an hour north. Leonard's daughters will not attend, as they haven't for four summers. They send him cards and talk to him on the phone (he is dying, after all), but they don't want to be around Betty, who finds them the oldest adolescent imbeciles she's ever encountered. Leonard announces that he will bring Sammy Two to Maple Run. Betty agrees with the idea; it will give them something to talk about other than Leonard's cancer.

How is Betty holding up?

She excuses herself from her bridge club and cries in Vanessa Murray's bathroom, three times in one night. She hangs up on a member of the prayer team. She flicks off Sammy Two when Leonard isn't looking.

What is the big surprise of the day at Maple Run?

That one of Leonard's daughters shows up with her family and surprises him and everyone, quite to the point of awkwardness.

But fortunately, Sammy Two saves the day by absorbing the attention of the grandkids (my how they've grown!) and allowing Betty to withdraw unseen for a solitary walk in the woods.

What does Betty think about on her walk?

That she needs to call her own daughter, who lives in Denver, and plan a visit. That she needs to send her son a birthday present, and that it's okay he doesn't want her to visit just now since he recently moved in with the girl whose name eludes Betty. That she misses Ted, her first husband. She misses how he used to call her Bethy, which was far too cutesy for a name, but a more perfect abbreviation of Elizabeth than the banal Betty. That perhaps she should not have married Leonard. That she is scared to death of Leonard dying.

What does Betty hear that makes her run back to the cottage faster than she has moved in years?

Leonard's voice—arched, howling—"Betty!" He is calling. "Betty! Oh Betty, I've killed him! Betty, where are you? I've killed him! Betty!"

What split-second moment will Leonard play over and over in his mind, in slow motion, until he can't take it anymore?

Not the moment of opening Sammy Two's cage, or the moment of Sammy Two eating a nut—rotating it round and round in his two paws—on Leonard's shoulder. Not the perfect undulating sine curve Sammy Two made as he ran along the wooden ledge of the screened-in porch. Not the moment of his grandchildren's laughter, or even the moment of Sammy jumping on Leonard's daughter's head, tousling her hair until she looked Leonard in the eyes and smiled warmly. Not the moment of holding Sammy Two's twitching, dying body in his hands as he stumbled off the porch calling for Betty. Or the moment of placing Sammy Two's still body into the fresh dirt at the foot of the maple tree (where, Leonard thinks sadly, he will have all the nuts he ever wants). And not even the improbable, impossible moment when Sammy Two darted up Leonard's chest, over his shoulder, then to the back of the solid green metal chair, which had a spring that allowed the back of the chair to move under Leonard's weight while Leonard made the backwards tilt that caused the solid green metal chair to press Sammy Two's body too hard—far too hard—and so fast—against the also green wooden frame of the screened-in porch.

The moment Leonard will remember is the one a few weeks before the picnic when it finally dawned on him that he was, in fact, going to die. He thought of his daughters as young, pigtailed girls chasing fireflies at dusk. He thought of his first wife helping them poke holes in the lid of the Ragu jar. He thought of Betty, of his inconsistent career-life. He thought of his fraternity brothers and teammates—the ones he'd lost touch with, the ones who had died, the ones he still saw every ten or fifteen years. He thought of heaven and wondered what it would possibly be like. And he thought, for the first time, of the actual moment of death (. . . *the cold of interstellar space, the absolute zero of Fahrenheit* . . .) and realized that he had never expected to die. He had always believed that Jesus would return before then. That he would get "taken up" to meet the Lord in the sky and reign with him forever and ever. But it hadn't happened yet, and was unlikely (even with the current political situation) to happen in the next 15 to 21 months. Leonard cried as he realized that he was actually going to die. Head in his hands, tears and snot streaming down his forearms. How had he been so wrong?

Then he felt the pressure of little feet on his back and shoulder, a paw touching his index finger. Leonard pulled his hand away from his face, sniffled, inhaled deeply to steady his breathing, and looked at Sammy Two, who was looking, with one large eyeball, straight into Leonard's wet eyes, just like the unblinking Jesus on that picture in the living room. In that moment, the one Leonard could not possibly have understood at the time but now plays over and over in his mind, Sammy Two held his gaze.

What can Betty feel in her fingertips as she embraces the inconsolable Leonard at Maple Run?

That the cancer is gone.

What does the doctor say at the next visit?

That the cancer is gone. He has a medical miracle on his hands.

So Leonard and Betty grow old together? Live happily ever after?

Leonard, exhausted, turns away from the God who has forsaken him, who has allowed Sammy Two to die and will—eventually—allow him to die. Whether of cancer or of old age, whether now or in twenty years, seems, ultimately, beside the point. He lives in his mind with Sammy Two on his shoulder, in his pocket, running ahead of him as they travel together along a narrow path toward Ithaca, where the Big Red team awaits them: linebacker and mascot. They follow the sound of the crowd cheering them on, the band trumpeting their imminent arrival.

Betty, on the other hand, is known to smile placidly and say to friends, to the prayer chain: "God works in mysterious ways." And she believes it. She comes to believe in a powerful and strange God.

KELCEY PARKER was born in Ithaca, New York. Her fiction has appeared in *Indiana Review, Image, Sycamore Review, Epiphany, GW Review*, and other journals. She has a PhD in Creative Writing and Literature from the University of Cincinnati, and currently lives with her husband and daughter in northern Indiana, where she is an assistant professor of English at Indiana University–South Bend.

Acknowledgments

Janice Daugharty, "Going to Jackson," © 2005. This story originally appeared in *The Ontario Review*. Reprinted by permission of the author.

Diane Glancy, "The Man Who Said Yellow," © 2006. This story originally appeared in *Image: A Journal of the Arts and Religion*. Reprinted by permission of the author.

Terry Hare, "The Flowers Fall," © 2007. Reprinted by permission of the author.

Michael Olin Hitt, "The Laying Out," © 2007. Reprinted by permission of the author.

Jerry B. Jenkins, "Midnight Clear," © 1992. This story originally appeared in *The Deacon's Woman and Other Portraits*. Reprinted by permission of the author.

Sally John, "Turn Right, Turn Left," © 2007. Reprinted by permission of the author.

Bret Lott, "The New Church," © 2007. Reprinted by permission of the author.

Thomas Lynch, "Block Island" © 2007. This story originally appeared in *The Southern Review*. Reprinted by permission of the author.

Kevin Macnish, "Isaac Laquedem," © 2007. Reprinted by permission of the author.

Andrew McNabb, "To Jesus' Shoulder," © 2007. Reprinted by permission of the author.

Michael Morris, "Last Chance Son," © 2007. Reprinted by permission of the author.

Kelcey Parker, "Ithaca," © 2006. This story originally appeared in *Image: A Journal of Religion and the Arts*. Reprinted by permission of the author.

A. H. Wald, "The Train to Ghent," © 2007. This story originally appeared in *The Southern Review*. Reprinted by permission of the author.

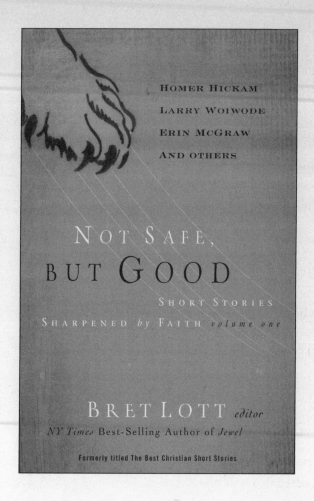

HOMER HICKAM

LARRY WOIWODE

ERIN McGRAW

AND OTHERS

NOT SAFE,
BUT GOOD

SHORT STORIES

SHARPENED *by* FAITH *volume one*

BRET LOTT *editor*

NY Times Best-Selling Author of *Jewel*

Formerly titled The Best Christian Short Stories

The first volume in a collection of contemporary

fiction that combines the artistry of critically acclaimed

writers with a clear Christian worldview.